DANNY ORLIS
AND THE
ANGLE INLET MYSTERY

By Bernard Palmer

Illustrated by
David Miles

D1197899

SWORD of the LORD PUBLISHERS

Post Office Box 1099•Murfreesboro, Tennessee 37133

All Scripture quotations are from
the King James Bible.

Printed and Bound in the United States of America

CONTENTS

Chapter One

DANNY'S NEWS

DANNY ORLIS, with his dog Laddie by his side, walked slowly to the corner. Danny looked up the highway for a glimpse of the International Falls Bus which should have pulled into Warroad, Minnesota an hour before.

"They'll be along in a minute, Laddie," he said to the mixed collie and shepherd dog beside him. His voice was tense with excitement. "They'll be along in a minute," he said again.

He could hardly wait to tell them what he had overheard coming out on the boat from American Point. He could tell them the thing that had sent the blood rushing to his cheeks and caused his spine to tingle with excitement, the thing that had kept him awake for half the night and even now set his heart to pounding. Treasure! And hidden in his own Angle Inlet territory! It was enough to make him excited. He looked up the street again, then turned and walked slowly toward the hotel. If only the twins would come!

Danny Orlis was not especially tall for all of his twelve years, but he was lean and wiry, strong as a hickory sapling and quick as a deer that inhabited his native Northwest Angle in Northern Minnesota. His face was burned brown from long months out of doors in the sun and rain. His eyes had already taken on a sharp, alert look, and he carried himself with the

1

easy grace of one who could walk or swim all day.

There was a dull rumble up the street, and Danny turned quickly to see the bus braking to a stop. Bob and Mike Lance were the first ones off. They took a step or two out onto the sidewalk, stopped, and looked nervously about. Danny would have known them anywhere.

"Hi," he called to them.

"Hi, yourself," Mike said.

Bob only grunted.

"Boy, I thought you two were never going to get here," Danny said as he picked up one of their suitcases and led them down the wide street toward the dock on Lake of the Woods. "The boat is due to sail at 8 o'clock. If we miss it we'll have to stay until tomorrow morning."

"That wouldn't be so bad," Bob said. "Even staying in this dump of a town would be better than going out in the—the wilderness where we're headed."

"Oh, you'll like it out at Angle Inlet," Danny said quickly. It was all he could do to keep from telling his secret now—but it wasn't safe out here on the street. Better wait until they were safely out on the boat, headed across the Lake of the Woods toward Oak and Flag Islands and Angle Inlet. "We've got the best fishing in the country and all sorts of big game."

"You can have them," Bob said. "I'll take St. Paul."

"Oh, don't pay any attention to him," Mike said, laughing. "He's just mad because Mom got sick and we had to come up here to the Northwest Angle to spend the summer with you."

"We could've stayed at home," Bob went on, "where we could have some fun. Why, I'll bet they

2

don't even have a show out where you live, Dan."

"A show?" Danny echoed. "Why, we don't have any roads or electricity or towns out on the Angle. I guess we don't have any shows." Then he added, "Of course I wouldn't go to them if we did have."

"You wouldn't go to a show?" Bob repeated. "Why not?"

"Well, you see," Danny told him, hoisting the suitcase into the lower deck of the boat, the *Bert Steele,* "I'm a Christian, and I feel it's better not to go to shows. There's so much drinking and gambling and sin in them."

"I never heard of such a thing as not going to shows," Bob said as he scrambled into the fisheries' boat after his brother. "But I might have expected that from a hayseed."

"What do you mean by being a Christian?" Mike asked.

"I mean that I've confessed my sins before God and put my trust in Jesus Christ to save me," Danny said, sitting down on the corner of a box of tools. "And because I'm a Christian I try to live as close to the way Jesus would want me to live as I possibly can."

"A Christian!" Bob snorted. "Sissy stuff."

"Aw, cut it out, Bob, will you?" Mike said. He was the taller of the twins, blond and good-natured, where Bob was dark-headed and sour.

"I've got a secret I want to let you in on," Danny whispered as they stood together at the ladder that led up to the top deck; "but we've got to be sure that we're alone before I can tell you."

Mike's eyes sparkled with excitement, but Bob was unimpressed. "What are you going to do?" he asked, "tell us that you know where an old mother rabbit has her nest?"

"You wait and see," Dan told him.

They climbed up the ladder and went to the back of the deck where they found a private corner away from the other passengers.

"Now what was this secret you were going to tell us?" Mike whispered.

"Well, I—" Danny began. But just then the captain of the *Bert Steele* called to him.

"Say, Danny, would you come down and move these suitcases for me? I've got a load of lumber and a couple of outboard motors that go out to Oak."

"I'll be back in just a minute," he said to the twins.

"I'll go," Bob said, getting quickly to his feet. "It's our stuff anyway."

Before Danny could protest, Bob had climbed down the ladder to the lower deck where the fish and freight were hauled.

"I wonder what came over him?" Mike said.

In a few minutes Danny heard his dog growl. "I wonder what's wrong with Laddie?" he asked.

"Sounds like he's got someone cornered," Mike said.

Laddie growled again, deep down in his throat. "It sure does sound like he's got someone cornered," Danny said, getting to his feet and starting toward the ladder. "He doesn't usually act like that."

Just then Bob screamed. "Danny! Get him off!" he cried. "Danny! Danny! He's killing me! Get me loose! Get me loose!"

Danny ran and descended the ladder to the lower

deck. There was Laddie holding Bob's hand between his teeth. The hair on the back of his neck was ruffed, and his long sharp teeth were bared. His jaws were trembling, and he was still growling.

"Get me loose, Danny!" Bob cried. "He's killing me!"

"Laddie!" Dan ordered sharply. "Laddie Boy. Come!"

The big dog looked at him appealingly, then loosed his hold on the frightened Bob and moved obediently to Danny's side.

"What's the matter, fella?" Dan spoke sternly to his dog.

"He tried to kill me. That's what he did. He tried to kill me."

"And if he'd been my dog," Captain Anderson put in, "I believe I'd have let him go. I saw how you kicked him in the face as you went by him."

Danny turned to his cousin, his eyes blazing. Bob took a step or two backwards, his face flushing.

"Don't you ever do that again," Dan said softly. "Don't you ever lay hands on my dog again."

Without saying a word Bob whirled and went back to the top deck. For several minutes he sat there rubbing his hand that Laddie had clamped down on. The dog's teeth hadn't broken the skin, but there were deep tooth marks that would be black and blue the next morning.

The big boat backed slowly away from the docks, turned and began to make her way slowly out of the harbor. There was a brisk wind blowing, and long, deep-troughed waves were rolling across the lake as the boat headed for Buffalo Point.

For a while the boys said nothing. Whenever

Danny would look at Bob, the city boy would turn away. There were several other passengers, fishermen or summer residents going out to the resort spots of the Lake of the Woods, but they gathered in the seats at the front of the boat, leaving the boys almost alone.

Finally Mike said, "Now what is that secret you were going to tell us?"

Danny leaned forward and lowered his voice. "On the way out on the boat last night I was almost asleep in the cabin when a couple of men came in and started to talk; I just couldn't help hearing what they said."

"Yes, yes, go on." Mike leaned forward until his head nearly touched Danny's. Even Bob moved in a little.

"The story goes back a long time ago, back to 1735 or so," Danny said softly, "to the time when old Fort Charles was manned by French soldiers, and the Dawson Trail from Angle Inlet to Winnipeg was being used."

"What's all that got to do with it?" Bob asked impatiently.

"Keep your shirt on, will you?" Mike exclaimed. "How do you expect Danny to tell us when you keep interrupting all the time?"

"Well, he starts to tell us what he heard a couple of guys say, and then he switches to a history lesson," Bob replied, scowling darkly. "What I can't figure out is, what's that got to do with it?"

"It has a lot to do with it," Danny went on, his voice in a hoarse whisper. "There was a lot of travel on the Lake of the Woods at that time. Men traveled over the Great Lakes to the northwest corner of Lake Superior, and canoed across to the Lake of the Woods, and then went across country on the old Dawson Trail to

Winnipeg. A lot of furs and gold traveled that route, and the Indians used to raid it every so often." He stopped a moment and looked around. "Those fellows said that there was one traveler about that time named Du Bois with an iron chest filled with gold coins—a whole fortune in them!"

Mike sucked in his breath sharply and moved a bit closer to Danny.

"This guy got as far as Fort Charles or Angle Inlet," Dan continued, "when word came of a terrible Indian uprising and massacre on the Dawson Trail. This Monsieur Du Bois got scared and buried his money!"

"On the Angle?" Mike asked excitedly.

"On the Angle or one of the islands, somewhere close by," Danny went on. "It couldn't have been far away because the Indians were so wild and hostile and Du Bois was so scared of them he wouldn't have gone far away, gold or no gold."

"Yes, but why didn't he come back and get it?" Bob asked.

"He was in a party that got ambushed and killed two days out of Winnipeg," Danny replied. "So his gold is still up here waiting for someone to come along and dig it up."

"That's right," Mike agreed, "but there's an awful lot of country it could be in. Finding it would be like finding a dime in a mountain of quarters."

"These fellows talked like they were looking for a map, or part of one. I heard them say that Du Bois had left a map to the treasure."

"Oh, boy," Bob exclaimed, his eyes shining. "Oh, boy! A real honest buried treasure!"

"S-s-sh," Danny put a warning finger to his cousin's

"Oh, boy! A real honest buried treasure!"

lips.

"Do you suppose there's any chance of us f-finding it?" Bob asked.

"We sure can look," Mike said.

Bob sighed deeply. "Boy, what wouldn't I do with my share if we find it? I'd buy me a hundred comic books and drink six dozen sodas and see fifty cowboy shows—" He stopped and turned to Danny, and said sneeringly, "Oh, excuse me. You don't go to movies, do you?"

"That's right," Dan grinned good-naturedly. "I don't go to movies or read comic books, either. Some of them are just about as bad as shows." He started to say more, but stopped abruptly. Two men were coming up the ladder from the lower deck. He grasped Mike's arm with a trembling hand. "It's them!" he said hoarsely. "I sure didn't expect to see them again. It's them!

Chapter Two

STRANGE GUESTS

DANNY ORLIS stared as the two strangers climbed the ladder to the upper deck and made their way forward. They lurched along, clutching their heavy suitcases and bracing themselves against the pitch and roll of the boat.

"It's them!" Danny repeated, the color leaving his face.

"Are—are you sure?" Bob asked.

"I know it's them," Danny went on, his voice quivering with excitement. "I'm positive! I'd know them anywhere!"

The strangers sat down just back of the cabin and began to talk immediately. They leaned close together, and every now and then one or the other would glance nervously about, as though to see whether they were being overheard. One of them was tall and angular with closely cropped black hair and a scar across one cheek that gave him a rough, hard-boiled appearance. The other was short and a roly-poly sort of man with thick lips and a shock of unruly blond hair that refused to stay under his hat.

"They're from the woods, aren't they?" Mike asked, looking at their mackinaws, their wool shirts and low-cut boots.

Danny shook his head. "Nope," he said, "they're

dudes, both of them. Look how sunburned they are. If they were from up here, they'd be burned brown by the weather. Then, too, their clothes are new, and their gear is new. You don't see anybody else aboard in new outfits, do you?"

"I guess you're right," Mike said.

"And look at those hunting knives they're wearing," Danny went on. "We never wear a hunting knife unless we're out in the woods or in a small boat on the lake. These fellows probably think they're fooling everybody, but they're not."

"What do you suppose they're talking about?" Bob asked.

"They must be talking about that treasure," Mike whispered, "from the way they keep looking around all the time."

"I'm going to slip up and see if I can hear what they're saying," Bob said, edging out of his seat.

"I could get over in the cabin and sit by that open window right next to them. And if they're talking about the treasure, I can really get a line on it."

"That's the idea," Mike said. "Maybe they'll drop a hint of where they're going to look for it or where they've got the map hidden."

But Danny shook his head. "No," he said, "we can't do that. We want to find the treasure as bad as they do, but it isn't honest for us to spy around and try to find out everything they know so we can beat them to it."

"But they've got a map to go by, and we don't have anything," Mike protested. "We don't have the slightest idea of where to begin, and that treasure could be buried anywhere."

"That's right," Danny said, "but I've got an idea that if we can find the right Indian we can find out a lot about it and where it could be buried. You know they've handed down a lot of things like that in stories from one generation to the next."

"And in the meantime they'll find the treasure and make off with it," Mike said.

"Talk about it not being honest to listen to them," Bob put in. "What isn't honest about it? It isn't against the law to listen to people talk."

"It might not be against the law to listen to them talk," Danny said, "but it certainly isn't Christian."

"You talk so big," Bob went on. "How did you find out about it in the first place if you didn't listen?"

"I just happened to hear what they were saying."

"What's the difference?"

"There's a lot of difference to me," Danny said.

The waves were higher now, and the stubby *Bert Steele* was lifting and falling heavily with each long, rolling breaker. Bob staggered along, clutching the rail, until he came opposite the cabin door. The men were so interested in their conversation they didn't hear him approach. Just as he let go of the rail and stepped towards the cabin, the *Bert Steele* lurched unexpectedly and caught Bob off balance. He staggered backward two or three steps and tripped over the strangers' suitcase, sending it sliding along the deck.

"The bag!" the tall one cried, clambering over the seat, as the suitcase scooted toward the lake. "Get it! Get it!"

By that time the short stranger had somehow climbed over Bob who was sprawled on the deck and threw himself across the suitcase as it teetered on the

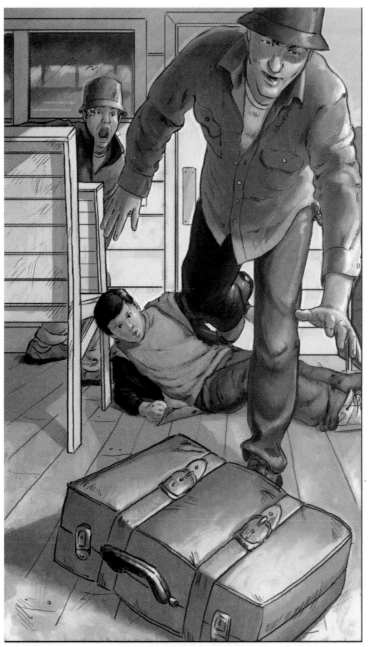

"The bag! Get it! Get it!

very edge of the boat, about to fall into the lake.

"I got it," the short one panted heavily. "I got it."

"Here, let me help you, Cliff," the tall stranger said, reaching down and taking his plump companion by the arm.

Sweat was standing out on Cliff's forehead, and his voice was trembling. I thought it was a goner," he panted, "but I got it. I got it." In a moment or two he turned on Bob who was just getting to his feet. "What was the big idea of snooping around us?" he demanded, his face coloring angrily.

"I—I was going to go into the cabin, and I—I lost my balance," Bob said lamely. "I'm s-sorry. I—"

"Aw, let him alone, Cliff," the other one said. "We've still got it. That's all that matters."

"Well, all right," Cliff said sullenly, "but if that suitcase had gone in the water, Bud, I'd have thrown you right in after it."

Bob hurried back to where Mike and Danny were sitting while the men took the suitcase back to their seats and put it between them on the deck.

"What happened, Bob?" Mike asked excitedly.

"Boy, I don't just know," he said, "but whatever they've got in that suitcase it means an awful lot to them."

In a moment or two the men looked back, stealthily.

"We'd better get to doing something," Danny whispered. "We can't be just sitting here staring at them."

He went up to the pilot house and borrowed Captain Anderson's binoculars, and they took turns scanning the coastline of the Northwest Angle for signs of moose or deer. First, Bob looked and then

Mike, and then Bob again. And every now and then they would give the glasses to Danny to have him identify something or other. They were so busy that they didn't notice the tall stranger approach them until he said, "Seeing anything, boys?"

They turned around quickly.

"N-n-no," Bob stammered. "We—we didn't see anything."

"We didn't mean to scare you like we did, Sonny," he went on. "My friend just lost his head for a minute." He smiled warmly, but Danny caught a hard, steel-like glint in his eyes.

"That's all right," Bob said.

"The skipper told me one of you boys lives at American Point," he said. "Can you tell me whether your dad has a cabin and a boat and motor we could rent for a couple of weeks?"

"Y-y-you mean you want to stay up there w-where we're going?" Mike asked.

"The fishing's good up there, isn't it?" the man asked.

"Why, sure," Danny put in quickly. "And I think Dad's got plenty of room. We don't have any guests at all now."

"That's fine. The Skipper said he thought it was safe enough for us to go out, but I thought I'd better ask you to make sure. Thanks." Then the stranger left them.

"He seemed friendly enough, didn't he?" Rick asked.

"Yes, he did," Danny answered, "but don't let that fool you. I think they're up to something besides finding that treasure, and I don't know what."

"What makes you say that?" Bob asked.

"It's just a hunch."

The boat was half an hour late into Oak Island because of the headwind, but the rest of the trip was in the island section of the lake where the waves were small, and the skipper made up the time with ten minutes to spare.

Mr. Orlis looked the strangers over carefully when they asked for a cabin. "I don't know," he said. "We have just a couple of cabins, and I'll have to put the boys in one."

"That's all right with us," Cliff said eagerly. "That other cabin will be just dandy."

"I'm not sure that I want to get myself filled up right now," said Mr. Orlis. Danny stood there holding his breath while his Dad weighed the matter in his mind. He knew that he was trying to size them up.

"We'd sure appreciate it if you could put us up for a while."

"Well, you can stay tonight, anyway," Mr. Orlis said, yielding.

The three boys carried their luggage out to the cabin and got situated before the bell clanged to call them in to supper.

There was a big crowd at the Orlis' table for the evening meal with the boat crew, the two strangers and the boys, to say nothing of a couple of the neighbors who had come over to pick up their mail. However, when they had finished eating, Mr. Orlis pushed back from the table and reached for his big, well-worn Bible on the radio behind him.

"It's our custom here to read the Bible and have a word of prayer every morning and night," he said,

15

opening the Bible to the Book of John.

That was one thing that Danny had to say about his dad. Everyone always said he was the bravest man on the Angle. He wasn't afraid of the storms on the Lake of the Woods, or the cold of the winters, or even of getting lost as he roamed the vast, roadless stretches of the Angle. And he wasn't afraid of what people thought about him for reading the Bible and praying. That was what he believed, and that was what he did.

That night he read the third chapter of John, where it tells how Nicodemus came to Jesus after dark and asked Him how to be saved. And Jesus told him that he would have to be born again.

It was a strangely interesting story to Bob who had never heard much of the Bible read before. He could picture the tall and stately Nicodemus coming down the dusty road at night to talk to Jesus. He could feel how mixed-up Nicodemus was when he asked the questions and tried to understand the answers. But, even though it interested him as few stories he had ever heard, he squirmed uncomfortably. What would those strangers and the captain of the *Bert Steele* think? What would those big burly neighbors think? He looked from one to another and was surprised to see that they were all listening as though they were as interested as he was. He tried to think of something else, but he could not. Everything his Uncle Carl was reading was aimed right at him. The words drove barbs into his heart. He was glad when the Bible reading and prayer were finally over and they were back in the cabin.

"I pumped Dad a little," Danny said as soon as the three of them were inside the cabin. "And he said that there have been fellows up here looking for the Du Bois' treasure off and on for years."

"Doesn't he think there's anything to it?" Mike asked quickly.

"Oh, he thinks there's something to it all right, but he thinks it's hid so well no one'll ever find it. It's a sort of laughingstock among the people who live up here."

"They'll probably laugh again when we find it for them," Bob said.

"Dad said he was about in the notion of sending those two men back in the morning; but he figured that if they were out here looking for the Du Bois' treasure, they're harmless enough."

"Did you get the names of any Indians to go see?" Mike asked.

"Oh, I already had them," Danny went on. "But say, I'd better go and talk to Dad about a boat or canoe for in the morning. I forgot all about that. Want to come along?"

As they stepped onto the porch of the main house, they heard Cliff say to Mr. Orlis, "There isn't any lock on the door of that cabin."

"Why, I don't even have a lock on my own house."

"Well, we want one for this one. Haven't you got a strong padlock and a hasp? We'll put it on."

Bob started to open the screen door, but Danny touched him on the arm.

"Why do you want your door locked?" Mr. Orlis went on. "Nobody ever steals anything around here."

"We want it locked, just the same. And we're going to fasten the windows shut, too!"

17

Chapter Three

A CALL ON RICK THUNDERBIRD

THE NEXT MORNING the boys were up and dressed and out on the dock beside the *Bert Steele* before anyone else was out of bed. The wind had died to a whisper, and the mirror-like creek was glistening in the early morning sun. From across the way the birds were singing, and, as they watched, a big fish leaped out of the water to spear a fly.

"Did you see that?" Mike asked excitedly. "Boy, did you see that big bass?"

"You'll see a lot of fish jumping before the summer's over," Danny laughed.

"Oh, boy!" Mike walked out to the end of the narrow dock. "It makes me want to get my rod and reel and start fishing."

"Any time you say," Danny told him.

"We're not going to do any fishing till we find that treasure," Bob put in.

Danny held a warning finger to his lips. "S-s-sh," he said softly. "The crew sleeps on the boat, and they might be awake."

"O.K.," Bob said sullenly. "I'll be careful, because I'm not going to give anything away." Mr. Smith, Danny's big gray tomcat, came up just then and rubbed against his legs. "Come on, kitty cat," he said impulsively, as he reached down and grasped the cat

19

about the middle. "You're going for a swim."

"Don't do that," Danny cried. But Bob had already thrown the cat out into the icy waters of the creek.

"What's the big idea, Bob?" Mike asked angrily, as Danny pushed past them to the end of the dock.

"I don't like cats," he said, laughing loudly, "unless they're swimming. Just look at him. Just look at him, would you? That's about the funniest thing I ever saw."

"There isn't anything funny about it," Danny snapped. He was on his knees at the end of the dock holding out his hands to Mr. Smith. "Come on, old man," he said. "Come on, buddy. Come on over here to me. I won't let him do that to you again."

When he had the trembling cat in his arms, he turned to Bob. His face was white and drawn, and his mouth was in a thin, hard line.

"I want to tell you something, Bob," he said so softly that Mike, who was standing close by, could scarcely hear him. "You can pull any kind of a joke you want to on me. I can take it. But you leave my pets alone. I've warned you once before. I'm not going to warn you any more. Understand?"

Bob's gaze fell before Danny's icy blue stare, and he turned and went shuffling off the dock.

Jack Crawford and Cliff Myers, the two strangers who had come in on the *Bert Steele* the evening before, were already in the house waiting for breakfast when the boys came in. Danny looked them over carefully. They were dressed in heavy wool clothes and had their hunting knives and fishing tackle on the porch.

"Yes, sir, we're all ready to go out after a big one," Jack, the tall, slender one, said. "And I'll bet you a dollar against a dime, Danny, that we get a bigger fish than you do."

Danny grinned at him. "I don't bet," he said, "but I usually do as well as the next guy when it comes to fishing here."

As they sat down to the breakfast table, Danny eyed the two men casually. There was something different about them this morning, something he couldn't figure out.

When they had all finished eating a big breakfast of steaming pancakes and golden syrup and oatmeal in cream so thick it clung to the spoon, Mr. Orlis took his Bible and began to read again.

"What do you do, Danny?" Bob whispered as they pushed their chairs back from the table, "read the Bible all the time?"

"Just at breakfast and supper," he answered.

The boys had Danny's chores done up in record time, filled the outboard motor with gas and shoved out into the creek.

"Where're we headed first?" Bob asked.

"I think our best bet is to go over to see Rick Thunderbird," Danny said. "He doesn't live very far away, and I think he might be able to give us some information about the map, or the treasure."

"Couldn't we fish on the way?" Mike wanted to know.

"No," Bob retorted, "we're not going to fish. We're going to stay after that treasure until we get it."

"O.K. but I'm sure hankering to get at those fish."

Danny opened the outboard motor to full throttle, and the light aluminum boat skimmed through the water. He went out of the wide-mouthed creek and turned northeast, threading among the islands that were scattered like marbles across the floor. They crossed over to the Canadian side of the Lake of the Woods.

"Boy, aren't you afraid of getting lost up here?" Mike asked as Danny banked sharply to the right and then to the left to go around a little blob of land that thrust its nose out of the water.

"I've been lost a few times," he admitted, "but I'm not lost now."

The twins looked about them eagerly. "Well, how do you like it, Bob?" Mike asked.

"They pray too much," he replied.

For an hour or more they twisted this way and that among the islands until Danny came at last to the little triangular strip of land at the mouth of Monument Bay where Rick Thunderbird had his cabin.

"Well, here we are," Danny said, cutting the speed. As they docked and got out of the boat, he continued, "I think it would be better if you'd sort of let me do the talking to him. He knows me a little, and I might be able to get something out of him. He's a funny old fellow and doesn't seem to like strangers too well."

The old Indian was sitting in his cabin by the fire when Danny knocked on the door. He grunted to them, and they went inside.

"Do you remember me, Mr. Thunderbird?" Danny asked.

The Indian nodded solemnly.

"We came over to see if you could help us with something," said Danny.

Rick Thunderbird reached over and put another

stick of wood in the barrel stove.

"Could you tell us anything about the Du Bois treasure that's supposed to be buried up here?"

"It happened a long time ago," Rick said gruffly. "A long time ago."

"I know, but did he leave a map or any directions telling where he buried it?"

The Indian reached out slowly and methodically stirred the fire.

"I know your people sometimes hand stories like that down from parents to children, and I knew that you would know if this story had been handed down that way."

Rick shook his head. "It was a long time ago," he said.

And, although Danny tried desperately after that, he could get no more out of the aged Chippewa Indian. Finally he got to his feet and shook hands with Rick and said good-bye.

"Well, what do you know about that?" Mike said as they walked down to the boat. "We couldn't get a single word out of him."

"No," Bob said angrily, "and the old fossil knows plenty about it too. You could see that in his eyes."

"If you could tell anything about him by looking at him," Danny said, "you're better than I am. I couldn't tell whether he knew anything or not."

They got in the boat, and Danny headed diagonally across Monument Bay. "I'm disappointed," he said. "I figured old Rick was our best bet."

"If he is, we don't have much chance of learning anything from the Indians," Bob said sourly.

"I thought he'd tell us what he could because he and Dad are pretty good friends. Dad's been trying to deal with him spiritually for a couple of years."

"Your dad's been trying to deal with him spiritually?" Mike echoed. "Just what do you mean?"

"He's been talking to him about his soul," Danny said.

"I still don't get you," said Mike.

"It's this way," Danny cut the throttle back to where he didn't have to shout to be heard above the motor. "We—you and I and Bob and Rick—and for that matter everyone in the world is born into the world with a sinful nature. The Bible tells us that there are none righteous, no not one, that no one seeketh after God, and that all we, like sheep, have gone astray."

"But what's that got to do with Rick Thunderbird?" Bob asked.

"It has a lot to do with Rick," Danny went on, "just like it has a lot to do with each one of us. Because the Bible tells us that the wages of sin is death.

"Since we're all sinners and the wages of sin is death, then it stands to reason that we've all earned death.

"Isn't that right?"

"I—I guess you're right," Mike said.

"C-can't you talk about something else?" Bob put in.

Danny didn't answer him as he went on, "If God had just left it all there, then there wouldn't be any hope in the world for anyone. But He didn't. He sent His Son, Jesus Christ, into the world to bear the sins of all. He'll save those who would put their trust in Him. It's like that verse Dad read last night, 'For God so loved the world, that he gave his only begotten Son, that whosoever believeth in him should not perish, but have everlasting life.' "

There was a long, tense silence. Bob stared at his feet, and Mike looked out across the water. "I—I never heard anything like that in my life before," the taller twin said.

"That's why Dad has been concerned about Rick. That's why I've been concerned about you."

"Well, you don't need to be concerned about me," Bob said harshly. "I'll get along all right."

At that moment Mike saw a canoe, half filled with water and washed up on the shore of a little island.

"Look!" he cried.

"Boy, there's a good canoe," Bob said. "Let's go and get it."

Danny turned the boat sharply and went back. "Why, that's old Rick's canoe," he said. "I'd know it anywhere."

"That doesn't make any difference. It's adrift. It

"Why that's old Rick's boat."

belongs to whoever finds it."

"Oh, no," Danny said, stopping the motor and coasting the boat up alongside the canoe. "It belongs to Rick. We'll have to take it back to him."

"Take it back to him?" Bob echoed. "After the way he treated us? I never heard of such a thing."

Mike and Danny dumped the water out of the canoe and fastened it to the stern of the boat with a light rope they happened to have along while Bob sat in the boat and sulked.

Old Rick had said but little to them when they were at his place the first time. He said little more the second time.

"I didn't know it was gone," he mumbled. "Must've got away during the windstorm yesterday afternoon."

As they left the old Indian's home, Bob turned to Danny once more. "That was the thanks we got from him," he said sharply. "We should've left the canoe out there instead of coming back with it."

They ate their lunch in the boat and visited three more Indians that afternoon. Two of them talked freely but knew nothing, and the third was like Rick Thunderbird. If he knew anything, he wasn't telling it.

When the boys finally got back to American Point, Danny's mother had begun to worry about them. "I'm so glad you're here, Danny," she said. "Now, if your dad and those strangers would only come, I'd be at ease again."

"Haven't they got back yet?" Danny asked.

She shook her head. "They went shortly after you did, and they were supposed to be back for dinner." Danny looked at Mike and then at Bob. It didn't sound good. It didn't sound good at all.

Chapter Four

BOB SKIPS CHURCH

AS SOON as the three boys were alone in their cabin, Mike said, "Boy, I hadn't even thought about your dad and those two guys not being back yet until your mom started worrying, Danny. What do you make of it?"

Danny crossed over to the bunk bed and sat down. "I don't know what to think," he said. "I don't think his staying out like this is anything to worry about. I've gone out with Dad when he said we'd be gone for a couple of hours, and we'd wind up staying all day."

"Yeah," Bob cut in, "but you didn't have a couple of bad apples like Jack and Cliff along. Why, they could clonk him over the head with a hammer and throw him in the lake, and no one'd know anything about it."

"That's just the way I've got it figured," Mike said. "Don't you think we ought to go out and try to find them?"

Danny got up and crossed over to the window and looked out. The sun was dropping behind the forest, and the shadows were creeping across Pine Creek.

"Do you s'pose we could find them if we did go out?" Bob asked excitedly. "Or do anything about it if we did find them?"

Danny turned around slowly, and both Mike and Bob eyed him as he walked over to the table and picked up his Testament. "I think the first thing to do is pray," he said slowly. "The Bible tells us that we should turn to Jesus when we have problems and troubles."

Mike and Bob just looked at one another, not knowing what to say.

"You—you mean that God will answer your prayer?" Mike asked. "Like if you pray, God will send your dad back home safe?"

"If it's in His will, yes," replied Danny.

In the silence that followed there was a low, even hum in the distance. "Listen!" Mike said suddenly. It was so faint at first that he could scarcely be sure he had heard it at all. But as they listened it grew louder and louder.

"It's a motor."

"And it sounds like Dad's new Lawson!" Danny exclaimed.

"A-a-are you sure?" Mike asked.

"Positive. There isn't another motor on this side of the lake that sounds like that one."

"That was quick answering on that prayer," Bob said, laughing scornfully.

"Yes," Danny told him in a voice so serious and earnest that it wiped the smile from the dark-headed twin's face. "Sometimes God answers our prayers even before we get them into words. I—I guess I've been praying in my heart ever since we talked with Mom, and she told us how worried she was getting."

While they stood there listening, the sound of the motor grew louder and louder until at last the dark, hulking shape of the boat came into view. A few minutes later the men came in laughing and talking loudly.

"Come on," Danny said, "let's go into the house. I want to hear what they've got to say."

"I never saw such fishing in all my life," Jack was saying as the boys went into the living room and sat down. "But what I really liked was getting a chance to look over the exact island where old Fort Charles used to be."

"Me too," Cliff Myers said. "Me too. We saw where the stockade used to be, and the cabins and the storehouses and the drill grounds."

"And tomorrow we're going to take a look at the cemetery. Aren't we, Carl?"

"Tomorrow's Sunday, Jack," Danny's dad said slowly. "And I've made it a policy never to work on Sunday."

"But we'll pay you for it," Cliff blustered. "We'll pay you good."

"That isn't the point," he went on. "Sunday's the Lord's day, and we try to keep it holy."

"Hmph," Cliff snorted. Jack Crawford changed the subject quickly.

A little later Bob began to squirm uncomfortably as Danny's mother brought out the dessert. In another couple of minutes Mr. Orlis would be reading the Bible again. Those words would be like so many swords thrusting into his heart. And every now and then Danny would look at him with clear blue eyes that seemed to look right into the very depths of his soul and see the sin and wrongdoing there. But they were as nothing compared to the prayers. For it was when they prayed that he was gripped the most. It was the prayers for righteousness and clean hearts that made him long so desperately to be rid of the weight of his own sins. It was the prayers for the lost that tore at him until he had to fight desperately to keep from yielding. He looked over at Jack and Cliff. What would they think if he lost his head and blurted out his need for salvation right before them all? No, he just couldn't risk it.

As soon as he had finished eating his pie, he excused himself and went outside. He could feel Danny's gaze upon him as he walked across the room and out the front door. He rather expected them to stop him, to ask him to come back and wait until the devotions were over. But they didn't. He was half disappointed as he stepped out onto the porch.

In a moment or two Cliff Myers got up and walked noisily to the door, without a word to anyone.

"I can't stand that stuff either," he said loudly, as he came outside. "This family'd be pretty much all right if it wasn't for all this Bible reading and praying. I don't see how they put up with so much religion."

"Me either," Bob said.

"Where'd you fellows go today?" the stubby stranger said casually as he leaned against a tall oak tree just a step or two off the porch.

"Oh, just around," Bob said.

"We're going to start digging tomorrow or the next day," Cliff said in a matter-of-fact tone.

"Y-y-you are?" Bob said, his heart jumping to his throat.

"Yeah, Jack thinks he's going to get some good specimens out of the old Fort Charles site."

"B-b-but how do you know you're going to find it there?" Bob asked.

"Oh, we'll find it all right," Cliff went on. "Our guide showed us right where it was, and it checked out with the map."

"It—it did?" Bob said.

"The university's been wanting to get some relics from Fort Charles and the old Hudson Bay town of Angle Inlet," Cliff went on. "So Jack and I came up to see what we could find during the summer vacation."

"Is that what you're doing up here?" Bob asked.

"Sure," he said, grinning at Bob. "What did you think we were doing?"

That night when the boys were in their cabin, Bob told Mike and Danny what Cliff had said. "They can't tell me that's what they're doing up here," Danny replied.

"Nor me," Mike said. "I think they believe that gold's buried over there where Fort Charles used to be, or maybe at the Hudson Bay town site. They're just using that university stuff to hide what they're really up to."

"I'll bet you're right, Mike," Bob told him, but Danny was not so sure.

"That could be, all right," he said. "But I just can't help thinking that there's more to this than just finding the treasure. I think the treasure's got something to do with it, all right. But I'm just sure there's something bigger behind it."

The next morning Mike and Bob went by boat with Danny and his folks over to church in the little schoolhouse. Bob hadn't wanted to go very bad and was the last one dressed and down to the boat.

"Do you suppose Cliff and Jack would want to go with us, Dad?" Danny asked.

"You could go see," his dad said. "We'll wait for you."

In a moment or two he was back. "They said they didn't think so this time, but maybe they'll go next week."

When they got out of the boat and started up to the schoolhouse to Sunday school, Danny hung back a little. "Do you know what Jack was doing when I went up to the cabin door?" he asked in a tense whisper.

Mike and Bob shook their heads.

"I could see him through the window. He had some sort of funny contraption about twice as big around as a stove lid and just about as flat. It had a long handle on it."

"What was it?" Bob asked excitedly.

"I don't know," Danny said, "but he jumped like he was shot when I knocked on the door."

Bob liked Dan's teacher from the start, even if he did try hard not to. He was a tall, grizzled trapper who had lost one eye in a bare-handed fight with a wounded bear.

Bob had never been in a Sunday school class quite like this one. One of the boys prayed and another read the Scripture lesson, and then everybody took turns answering and asking questions. The teacher didn't say very much; but when he did, it really meant something.

"You know, some boys think they're smart in doing things that the world does," he said in summing up the lesson. "They think they're really somebody when they stick a cigarette in their mouths, or lie, or tell dirty stories. But you know anybody can do those things. They can teach a monkey to put a cigarette in his mouth. The thing that takes courage and real strength of character and really shows that you are a man, is to be able to say "No, I've taken Jesus Christ as my personal Saviour, and it's better for a Christian not to do those things.'"

Bob looked out the window. Why was it that everywhere he went the things that were said twisted and tore at his heart? He had to get out of there, or he was going to make a fool of himself.

As soon as Sunday school was over, Bob said to Danny, "Is there any way of getting back to your place except going by boat?"

"Sure, we walk to school through the woods all the time," Danny said. "That trail over there leads right to our house." He pointed to a narrow twisting path through the trees.

"How far is it?"

"Oh, about a mile and a half. Why?"

"I'm not going to sit through another stuffy church service today," Bob said. "I'll be seeing you when you get back." With that he ran out of the schoolhouse toward the trail. Danny called to him but he did not stop.

Bob ran along the trail for two or three hundred yards, twisting and turning among the trees before he stopped to look back. It was dark in the forest, so dark that it seemed to Bob that the sun had suddenly gone down, leaving only the faint half-light of evening. It was quiet too. He could hear his own heavy breathing and the beating of his heart. He looked about him quickly, as though he was suddenly afraid some ferocious animal was about to pounce on him. But there was nothing. Not even a rabbit or a chipmunk! Why, there wasn't anything in the woods to scare anyone. It was just an idea a fellow got. The woods were as safe as the streets in Minneapolis—safer maybe.

Bob began to feel better as he walked along. This

There stood a huge, towering moose!

was fun—a lot better than being back there in church hearing—he stopped suddenly. His eyes bugged wide, and his mouth dropped open. There on the path ahead of him stood a huge, towering moose!

The sweat came out on Bob's forehead, and he began to tremble. He tried to move, to turn and flee before the great beast charged him; but for an instant he could not. He stood there as though he had grown roots like the trees, roots that held him captive and would not let him go. The moose, who had caught wind of Bob about the same time Bob spotted him, held his head high. His massive rack of horns was in the tree branches, and his whole body was tense and quivering. Bob tried to cry for help, to scream for Danny or Mike or anyone, but the sounds were stuck in his throat.

Chapter Five

RICK RETURNS THE CALL

BOB LANCE was rooted to the ground. The great hulking moose was standing about ten yards away, with his head high, his nostrils quivering and his eyes riveted on the boy. Suddenly Bob found his voice and his legs. He let out a long, piercing scream, turned and raced back down the narrow, crooked path at top speed. At any moment he expected to hear the thunder of hooves behind him, to feel the moose's hot breath on his neck and those heavy horns in his back. He ran harder and harder. Then he slipped and fell down over a dead birch log, but he scrambled to his feet and began to run again. He had been too frightened to hear the big moose snort with terror and go charging off through the woods in the opposite direction. Though he ran until he thought his lungs would burst, he didn't stop until he reached the little clearing and the schoolhouse.

For a couple of minutes he stood on the porch, his breath coming in long, rasping gasps. There was sweat on his forehead, and his hands were skinned and bleeding. He went down to the lake and washed himself as best he could, then went into the schoolhouse and sat just inside the door. The minister, one of the settlers who lived close by, had just begun to talk.

When the service was over and everyone had filed

outside, Danny came over and said, "Why, Bob, I thought you went home."

"Nope," Bob said. The color came up in his cheeks. "I changed my mind."

As the light aluminum boat turned into the creek where they lived, Danny saw a canoe pulled up on shore.

"Look," he said, "we've got company."

"I guess we have," Bob exclaimed, pointing to a tall, dark figure standing on the dock. "It's that old Indian we went to see. It's old Thunderbird himself."

"It is, for a fact," Danny's dad said. "Old Rick hasn't been over here for months. I wonder what brought him this time."

"I want to see the young one," Rick Thunderbird said when Mr. Orlis stopped to talk with him.

"Do you mean Danny?"

"I mean him," the Indian said, pointing to Danny. "I want to talk to him."

"Why, sure. Danny!" Mr. Orlis called. "Come on over here. Rick Thunderbird wants to talk to you."

"Someplace where the walls do not have ears," the old Indian said pointedly.

"Let's go out to our cabin, then," said Danny.

Danny and Thunderbird and Mike and Bob walked single file to the log sleeping cabin. When the door was closed, the old Indian said, "You brought back my canoe."

"That's right," Danny told him. "We found it washed up on another island and figured that it must've gotten away from you in a storm."

"I knew we shouldn't have taken that canoe back,"

Bob whispered softly to Mike. "Now we're in the soup."

"Rick would have starved, maybe, without his canoe," the Indian went on, talking about himself as he would someone else. "No one ever stops to see him, and it's months till the lake freezes over."

"We knew you couldn't get along without your canoe," Danny said.

Rick nodded solemnly. "You brought Rick's canoe back," he went on, "after he had sent you away without answers to your questions. That is not the way of the white man—or the Indian either."

"It's the Christian way, Mr. Thunderbird," Danny said. "The Bible tells us that we should do unto others as we'd like to have them do to us."

"Your father, he tell me about being Christian," the old Indian said. "He tell me how it makes a man love his neighbors, how it makes him good and kind, how it makes him live clean and honest. But I not see that in any besides your father. I think maybe it not for me." Thunderbird sat down on the side of the bunk next to Bob and clenched his long, gnarled fingers nervously. "But you bring back my canoe. That's the first kind thing anyone besides your father ever do for Rick." He got up and hobbled over to the chair beside the window. "All night I could not sleep, young one. I think about this thing you do for a poor old Indian. I think about this Jesus I knew had caused you to do it. I want to know this Jesus who makes you so kind."

Bob stared at old Thunderbird as though he could scarcely believe what he had heard. Here was a hard, bitter old Indian who had been a chief in his younger days—an Indian chief who had fought against the whites and resisted every effort to be put on a reservation, a chief who preferred to suffer hardships and hunger and cold rather than bow to the white man's will. And yet he was talking of his need for Christ Jesus as his personal Saviour. It was enough to tear at Bob's heart with claws of steel.

"Well," Danny said, fumbling with his Testament, "the Bible tells us that first of all we've got to realize that we're sinners and need a Saviour."

"Sinners?" Rick asked. "What do you mean?"

Mike moved quietly to the bed and sat down while Danny turned to the third chapter of Romans. "The Bible explains it a lot better than I can," he said. "Here in the tenth verse of the third chapter it says, 'As it is written, There is none righteous, no, not one.' And down in the twenty-third verse of the same chapter, 'For all have sinned, and come short of the glory of God.'" Danny stopped a moment, struggling for words. "That means that everyone, you and me and Rick and Bob here—all of us have sinned. We've all done things we shouldn't do, things that we know are wrong; but we go right ahead and do them anyway. I guess the only way you can explain it is that we're just naturally wicked."

Rick nodded solemnly. "One who has lived all his life in sin well knows that his heart is evil." Rick Thunderbird's eyes were clear and his voice steady. But Danny could tell by the serious look on his face that he was thinking of those things he had done which were sinful in the eyes of God and man.

"If God had just left it there," Danny said, "there wouldn't be any hope for any of us. But He didn't. He gave a remedy for sin." The sandy-haired boy turned to his Testament again. "'For God so loved the world, that he gave his only begotten Son, that whosoever believeth in him should not perish, but have everlast-

40

ing life.' Jesus gave Himself for us."

"Gave Himself?" Rick asked pointedly. "How He give Himself?"

"The Bible tells us that Christ died for our sins according to the Scriptures; and that he was buried, and that He rose again the third day according to the Scriptures," Danny continued. "That is the way Jesus gave Himself for us so we can have eternal life if we just put our trust in Him."

"God sent His Son for me?" the old Indian repeated slowly. "For old Rick Thunderbird?"

"That's right."

There was a long, painful silence. Once or twice Danny started to speak, but did not. Instead he waited until finally Rick said softly, "I—I—don't know how to pray."

"But you don't need to know how," Danny said quickly. "I don't think God pays much attention to the words, anyway. The important thing is to pray with your heart."

He asked old Rick to kneel, and Danny taught him the prayer of the sinner, "God be merciful unto me a sinner." When at last they got to their feet, there was a wide smile on Thunderbird's wrinkled face.

Without saying a word he took Danny's hand and squeezed it warmly.

Bob and Mike looked at one another and then back at the aged Indian chief and their wiry young cousin. Bob felt his lower lip quiver, and he turned suddenly away. If only he had the courage old Thunderbird did!

"Danny," Mike said, his voice choking strangely and his lips scarcely forming the words, "sometime I want to talk to you—alone."

"Why, sure, Mike," Danny said. "Can't we talk now?"

Danny excused himself for a moment and went into the house. As he went out the door, Bob said to his twin brother, Mike, "What's the matter, Pantywaist? Are you going soft on me?"

"Oh, keep still," Mike snapped, and turned away.

"You should not fight with Jesus," Rick said evenly. "For eight year I fought Him, and not until today am I happy."

Danny came back just then with a well-worn leather Bible. "You take this, Mr. Thunderbird," he said. "It's my Bible, and it's sort of marked up; but you can keep it to read until you get one of your own."

"You mean you give me this Bible?" Rick asked.

Danny nodded, smiling. It was the Bible his mother had given him for Christmas two years before, but Rick had to have a Bible. He had to have God's Word so he could read and study.

"But, my young one," Rick said, "old Thunderbird never go to school. He don't know how to read."

"Then I'll come over and read to you every once in a while. How'd that be?"

For answer Rick reached out his hand and shook Danny's hand.

Mr. Orlis came out presently and suggested that Rick stay and visit awhile, and the boys take him home in the boat toward evening.

"Yes," Rick said, "I have much to talk with you about."

When the two men were gone into the house, Danny said, "Wasn't it wonderful that Rick

"God sent His Son for Me?"

Thunderbird took Christ as his Saviour today? We've been praying for him at family devotions for a couple of years."

"I don't know what was so wonderful about it," Bob said shortly. "He's nothing but a dumb Indian."

"In God's sight," Danny replied, "he's more than just a dumb Indian. He's just as important as you are or I am."

"Do you know something?" Mike put in suddenly. "Jack and Cliff haven't stuck their noses outside their cabin all day, except to go in and eat breakfast."

Danny looked out the window at the cabin across the way. "That's right, and they've got the blind drawn tight. There's something going on, fellows, something more than just a treasure hunt."

"You might be right," Mike said. And, dropping his

voice to a whisper, he went on. "I'll bet they're working with that funny-looking machine you saw this morning, Danny."

Just then Jack came out onto the porch and looked around. Danny let go of the curtain and stepped back quickly. Mike and Bob pressed close beside him, peering out through the thin curtain at the stranger on the porch of the neighboring cabin.

"Those guys are scared to death they're being watched," he said. "There's something going on over there. I think we ought to get to the bottom of it."

"Me too," Mike said.

"But how?"

"That's what I want to know," Bob put in. "I tangled with that Cliff once, and I—I thought he was going to knock my head off."

"That's right," Danny went on. "Whatever we do we've got to be careful."

"B-b-but what if we get caught?" asked Bob.

"We'd just better not get caught," Danny replied.

Chapter Six

SEARCH BEGUN

DANNY, BOB AND MIKE sat together in the little one-room cabin looking at one another. Danny was toying absent-mindedly with a short piece of rope he had picked up off the floor.

"Boy," Mike said. "I'd give a lot to know what Cliff and Jack are really up to."

The young woodsman tied a bowline in the piece of rope and untied it slowly. Then he said, "You know, I think we ought to go over and pay those two guys a visit."

"You mean g-g-go right in their cabin a-and talk to them?" Bob asked.

"Sure, why not?" Danny said.

"B-b-but there's n-n-no telling what they'll do if they get on to us," Bob went on, stuttering in his excitement. "And believe me, they're plenty t-t-tough! I know!"

"We won't be doing anything except paying them a little social visit," Danny explained. "They can't do anything about that. And we can get some straight dope that way. All we have to do is to go in and talk to them about fishing and the lake, and stuff like that, and really keep our eyes and our ears open."

"Well," Bob said, "I'll go, if you'll do the talking."

"What's on your mind, Boys?"

"O.K.," Danny replied, "let's go."

When they were just outside the cabin door, Danny whispered, "Let's be as quiet as we can going up on the porch. Maybe we can get a look at something through the window like I did this morning."

They stepped quietly onto the porch and up to the door. The blind was drawn tightly, but by stooping a little Danny could see inside. He sucked in his breath sharply and straightened up so suddenly that it startled Mike and Bob.

"What's the matter?" Mike whispered tensely. "What'd you see?"

Without speaking Danny stooped again while his companions stood there trembling. After a moment or two he straightened once more and knocked firmly on the door.

There was a scurrying inside. The sound of sliding chairs and crumpling papers, and the heavy thud of something being thrown under the bed came to them through the closed door.

Danny knocked again.

"Just a minute," Jack called. "We'll be with you in a minute."

There was a long, tense silence.

"Come on," Bob whispered. "Let's get out of here!"

But Danny grasped him by the arm. "S-s-sh," he cautioned, "or you'll give it all away."

It was another couple of minutes before Jack came to the door. He opened the heavy, homemade door just wide enough so he could see who was there. "What's on your mind, Boys?" he asked. He was careful to stand squarely in the way so they couldn't see into the cabin.

Danny eyed him critically. It seemed to him that Jack was pale and that a thin line of sweat stood out on his forehead. "We came over to visit a little while," Danny said. "We didn't have much to do."

"I'll tell you, fellows," Jack said. "Cliff's got a busting headache. You'd better come back tomorrow." With that he closed the door and bolted it on the inside.

"Well, what do you know about that?" Bob exclaimed.

"I'll tell you, though," Danny said loudly. "A bad headache isn't anything to laugh about. It can really lay a fellow out." With that he took Bob and Mike by the arm and hurried them off the porch and down the narrow lane. "They'll be watching us," he said softly. "Act like we're just fooling around."

They stopped at the boat that was tied to the dock in front of their cabin and bailed the water out of it, then sauntered over to where Danny's dog, Laddie, was lying. Mike threw a stick, and the dog went bounding after it.

"What'd you see?" Bob asked excitedly. "What'd you see over there?"

"I—I don't know for sure," Danny told him. "That funny contraption I saw this morning was in a corner half covered up with a piece of canvas. And both Jack and Cliff had some big square piece of paper that looked awful old, and they were drawing something on the paper."

"Drawing something?" Bob echoed. "What could they find up here to draw? Especially inside like that and with all the blinds pulled! I always thought an artist had to be looking at what he was drawing."

"What they were drawing is just what I don't know

for sure," Danny went on. "But it looked an awful lot like they were making maps."

Mike and Bob both stared at him. "Making maps!" Mike repeated. "What would they be making maps for?"

"That's something we've got to find out," Danny went on slowly. "When a fellow hunts for treasure he *follows* a map. He doesn't draw one."

They all three looked at one another, and then over at the little sleeping cabin where the mysterious strangers were staying.

In a few minutes Mr. Orlis came out and told Danny that Rick Thunderbird was ready to go back home.

"Would you get the gas, Mike?" Danny asked as he lashed Rick's canoe to the aluminum boat securely with a piece of strong rope. "I think we'll need a little more gas than what's in the tank to go clear over to Monument Bay."

Both Mike and Bob went for the gas while Danny pulled the boat and canoe alongside the dock and held them until Rick got in.

The old Indian was smiling broadly, but he did not say much until they were almost to his island. "I tell your dad about Rick finding Jesus," he said.

"That's fine," Danny replied.

"You come over and read to Rick by-and-by," Thunderbird went on. "You read him the Bible so he know how to live and what to do."

"Sure," Danny grinned.

"You won't forget?"

"No," the young woodsman said, "I won't forget."

"Now, Rick going to do something for you." The

smile faded from the Indian's face. "You asked Rick about map and treasure. Rick say he not know what you talk about. I lie. For long time I know, but I vow never to tell white man. But Rick tell you, because you help Rick find Jesus."

Danny cut the speed of the motor so he could hear the aged Indian's low voice, and Bob and Mike crowded close, listening breathlessly.

"Old Gibb McCloud say he have map," Rick Thunderbird said. "Before he die he say he have map. And Gibb always tell truth."

"You mean the old Gibb who used to live on Harrison Creek? The one who died last fall?"

Thunderbird nodded seriously.

"Are you sure?" Mike asked, his voice tense.

"Gibb was honest," he said simply.

"Do you know where he kept it?" Danny asked. "Did you ever hear Gibb say?"

"No," the old Indian said, shaking his head. "That is for you to find."

"But if you knew he had it," Bob blurted, "why haven't you gone looking for it?"

Rick stared at him momentarily. "What would I do with gold?" he asked.

When they had finally started back toward American Point, Bob said excitedly, "Now we've really got something to go on."

"That's right," Danny said. "And, believe me, we'll get down to Gibb's old place on Harrison Creek the first thing in the morning. This is really a good break."

"Yeah," Bob said, "if Rick wasn't stringing us along. You don't suppose he was, do you?"

"No," Danny said. "Rick wouldn't do that, especially now that he's a Christian."

"Oh, now, that isn't going to make so much difference in that old Indian," Bob said, scoffing. "I know he gave out with the secret of the map a little while ago, but that was because he's still a little soft from you working on him with that religion stuff. He'll be as ornery as ever tomorrow."

Before Danny could reply, Mike said seriously, "No, Bob, I don't think so. Something happened to old Rick Thunderbird today. I—I don't know for sure just what it was, but he's different, and he's going to stay different. I'd almost stake my life on that."

"That's right, Mike," Danny said. "The Bible tells us that when we're born again we become new creatures in Christ. That's what happened to Rick. And that's what can happen to you and Bob if you'll only let Jesus come into your hearts."

Both of the boys looked away quickly, and for a long while they were silent.

The next morning was blustery and cold with a biting west wind and just a hint of rain that every now and then skipped in great droplets across the water. The boys had planned on getting an early start for Gibb's deserted cabin over on Harrison Creek in spite of the threatening weather, but Mr. Orlis had some work he wanted them to do. It was almost noon before they finished with it.

"Well," Danny said, as they filed out onto the dock, "I guess we're all set for Gibb's place."

"Yeah," Bob said disgustedly. "We're all ready, and your dad's got one motor torn apart and the other one out on the lake. We can't go anywhere."

"Sure we can," Mike said. "We can row."

"Row, humph! That's work," said Bob.

"It's too far to row a boat," Danny put in, "but we can take the canoe and paddle."

"I don't see why he couldn't have picked some other time to tear that outboard motor apart," Bob muttered to himself as they got into the canoe.

"We're headed for that treasure map," Mike said softly, his voice tense with excitement. "That's the main thing. I'd be happy even if we had to walk."

"Me, too," Danny said.

"Do you suppose we'll find it?" Mike asked as Laddie jumped nimbly into the canoe and lay on the bottom with his soft nose touching his young master's knee. "Really find it, I mean?"

"I—I think we will, if somebody else hasn't beat us to it," Danny replied.

Although they paddled as fast as they could, it was almost two hours later that their canoe touched shore in front of Gibb's deserted cabin. For a couple of minutes the boys stood there looking about, without speaking.

All the windows had been broken out of the little square house, the porch was leaning badly and the back door was hanging by one hinge. The woodshed was in even worse repair, and the roof on the barn had fallen in.

"Boy," Mike said, "it doesn't look like there could be any treasure map here, does it?"

"Well, come on," Bob said excitedly. "Let's get going. This place gives me the creeps."

"I think we'd better go through the house first," Danny said. "He'd be most apt to hide the map in the house."

"H-how long did you say it has been since old Gibb died?" Bob asked as they stopped on the porch.

"I can't remember exactly," Danny said.

"Where'd they bury him?" Mike put in.

"Over on the hill—" Danny began. But his voice choked off suddenly. "What's that noise?" he asked.

Chapter Seven

MIKE MAKES A DECISION

"WHAT'S THAT?" Danny asked again. For a moment or two the boys stood there beside the ramshackle old house, listening. "It—it sounds like an outboard motor," Bob said hoarsely.

Danny took a step or two toward the wide stream.

The low, throbbing hum was louder now. There was no mistaking it. It was an outboard motor coming toward them, fast.

"Somebody's coming!" Danny exclaimed, starting to run toward the water's edge. "We've got to get that canoe out of sight."

"T-there isn't time," Bob said, looking wildly about as though he was searching for a place to hide. "We—we'll never make it!"

"What do we want to hide for?" Mike wanted to know. "We haven't done anything."

"No," Danny explained as he jumped nimbly into the canoe and reached for the paddle. "But we're hot on the trail of the Du Bois map. If we're caught snooping around over here, somebody's apt to get wise."

"Yeah," Bob said, "and if that somebody happens to be Cliff and Jack, it might be too bad for us, besides."

"Do—do you really suppose it's them?" Mike asked.

"It sure could be," Danny told him, paddling the canoe downstream a dozen yards or so to a thick clump of brush that grew out over the water. "That sounds an awful lot like a Lawson motor. And Dad's the only one who has one on this side of the lake."

"They—they wouldn't really do anything to us with your dad along," Bob stammered uncertainly. "Would they, Danny?"

"Of course not."

"But Uncle Carl won't be with them all the time," Mike put in. "If they were to see us here, they might dope something out and wait until they catch us alone. That's the thing that's got me worried."

"Well, don't just stand there. Do something!" Bob cried. "They're just around the bend! Hurry up!"

Danny was working rapidly but calmly. He tied the light rope securely to a small tree so the current wouldn't sweep the canoe away, pulled the branches down over the trim craft to hide it completely and scrambled to his feet. "There," he said. "That's done."

"Come on!" Bob shouted. "They'll be here in a minute!" He was already halfway to the house.

Mike and Danny started to run toward the dilapidated old barn with Danny's dog, Laddie Boy, right beside him.

"This way!" the young woodsman shouted. "If they stop here at all, the house'll be the first place they'll go!"

The three of them crowded through the narrow barn door and, breathing heavily, flopped onto the rotting hay.

"We made it," Bob gasped. "We made it."

Danny placed his finger across his cousin's mouth

in warning. Bob scowled and pulled away. For a couple of minutes he lay there without speaking, his breath coming in long, dry gasps. Laddie seemed to sense what was happening and pressed close to Danny, his soft nose finding his master's hand.

"Whoever it is, is stopping out front," Mike whispered as the sound of the motor quit abruptly.

"I'm going to take a look," Danny said, getting to his feet and moving cautiously toward the broken out window in the corner of the barn. "It's them!" he whispered. "It's Dad and Cliff and Jack! And they're headed this way!"

"What do you suppose they're doing?" Mike asked in a hoarse whisper.

"Looking around, maybe," Danny said.

"Hunting for the treasure map, maybe," Bob put in.

While they lay there on the hay scarcely daring to breathe, they could hear the three men get out of the boat and walk noisily up toward the house.

"The old Dawson trail starts right back of Gibb's homestead here," Danny's dad was saying loudly as they walked past the barn. "It goes from here across country to Winnipeg. Used to be a right famous trail a couple of hundred years ago. Guess there was a heap of travel on it then."

"Do—do you think they'll come in here?" Bob managed to whisper.

Danny shook his head.

While the boys listened, the voices got softer and softer and softer until finally they couldn't hear them anymore.

"Will they have to come back this way?" Bob asked after five minutes of breathless waiting. "No," Danny said. "They'd go back there to look at the Dawson Trail, and then Dad would probably take them over to see old Gibb's grave. That'd take them way west of us."

Even as he spoke the outboard motor came to life.

"There," Bob said, sighing deeply. "They've gone at last." He would have gone outside, but Danny stopped him.

"We'd better give them time to get out of sight," he said. "One of them might happen to be looking this way."

When the sound of the motor had died to a whisper, the three boys and Laddie Boy left the barn and started toward the house.

"Now where do you imagine old Gibb would've hidden that map?"

The house looked as though a tornado had gone through it.

"I don't know," Danny said, "but it doesn't look like we're the only ones who've been here looking for it."

The little three-room house did look as though a tornado had gone through it. The dishes and utensils were scattered about the kitchen. The stove lids had been thrown on the floor, and the pipe had been jerked out and thrown to one side. The bedroom and living room had received the same treatment. Old Gibb hadn't had much furniture, but the little he'd had had been torn apart. The thin cotton mattress had been slashed in a hundred places with a sharp knife, and cotton was strewn across the floor. The hollow iron bedstead had been hacked in pieces, and the horsehair couch had been ripped up. A couple of faded old pictures in battered frames had been torn from the wall and thrown in the corner.

"Maybe somebody's already found it," Bob moaned when he saw how things were.

"Nope," Danny countered. "They wouldn't have torn the house up like this if they had.

"Maybe so," Mike said. "But it's sure going to be a rough deal finding it in this mess. It looks like every decent hiding place has already been raided."

They poked around in the house a little, and went through the barn and woodshed. But the searchers had been there as well. Boards had been jerked off, boxes and barrels had been pried apart, crockery jars had been broken. Every inch of every building had been carefully gone over.

"You don't suppose Cliff and Jack have been over here before today, do you?" Bob asked as they came out of the barn and stood looking down on the spot where the canoe was hid.

"It could be," Danny said.

"Well," Mike added, "whether it was Cliff and Jack or someone else, it's getting pretty late. I think we ought to be starting back."

Danny squinted at the clouds that were churning over the trees. "It's going to cut loose and rain tonight," he said, "but I believe we've got time to look in one more place."

"Where's that?" Bob asked.

"At old Gibb's grave."

"His grave?" the boys echoed.

Danny nodded.

"Oh, no," Bob said. "Not me. I'm not looking in any grave. Treasure or no treasure!"

"We'll look around it, anyway," Danny said, laughing.

The three of them, with Laddie padding along beside, walked through the woods to a small weed-infested clearing. The only sounds were those of their feet crackling branches and dry grass and their labored breathing. Danny stopped on the edge of the clearing and pointed to a weather-beaten little house about twice the size of a doll house resting on a long, narrow mound. "There it is," Danny said softly.

"What kind of a grave is that?" Mike asked.

"It's just a regular pagan, Indian grave," Danny told him. "You see the Indians have some funny ideas about God and Heaven. They have sort of a belief in Heaven, but they don't think God, or the Great Spirit as they call their god, has much power. If they bury a body in a casket or box, they always drill three holes in it so the soul can get out. Then they put a little house on the grave with some tobacco and food in it."

"What's that for?" Mike asked, his deep brown eyes serious.

"I'm not sure," Danny said, sitting down on a big rock. "But I think they build it so the soul will have a place to live."

"Then the food must be for the soul to eat," Mike said.

"That's a lot different than what the Bible teaches us," said Danny. "The Bible teaches us that Jesus said to His disciples, 'In my Father's house are many mansions: if it were not so, I would have told you. I go to prepare a place for you. And if I go to prepare a place for you, I will come again, and receive you unto myself; that where I am, there ye may be also.' A Christian doesn't have to depend upon a little wooden house nailed together by his friends and relations as a resting place for his soul. He has a home which God has prepared for him. God prepared a place in Heaven for those who put their trust in Him, just as there's a place in Hell for those who haven't taken Him as their Saviour."

"You—you don't believe that everybody is going to go to Hell, do you?" Mike asked. His face was drawn and white as he asked the question.

"I believe what the Bible says," Danny told him. "And the Bible says that everyone who refuses to confess his sins and take Christ as his Saviour will go to Hell."

There was a long, heavy silence. "I—I can understand about somebody like—well, like old Gibb who maybe drank a lot, or someone who steals or cheats or lies," Mike said at last. "But what about the good people?"

Danny flipped open his Testament to Romans 3:10.

"The Bible tells us," he began. " 'There is none righteous, no not one. There is none that understandeth, there is none that seeketh after God.' And in another place it says, 'The wages of sin is death.' That means that everyone is wicked enough to be cast into Hell before he has accepted Jesus as his Saviour, whether he tries to be good or not."

"Do you think that means me, too?" Mike asked. He spoke so softly Danny could scarcely hear him.

Praying that God would give him the right words to say, Danny said, "Yes, Mike. It means you and anyone else who hasn't taken Jesus Christ into his heart. Three or four years ago it meant me too. But I took advantage of God's grace and mercy. I made it right with Him by taking Christ as my Saviour."

For two full minutes Mike stared at the ground. Finally he raised his eyes.

"Would you show me the way to let Christ into my heart?" he asked.

Rejoicing, Danny knelt with Mike right there in the woods. Danny explained the way of salvation again, as clearly as he possibly could. He told Mike how he must confess his sin before God and how he must completely and absolutely place his trust in Christ who died on the cross and arose from the grave that men and women and boys and girls might be saved. He told him how he must be ready to forsake anything that should stand in the way between himself and Christ. As they prayed they forgot Bob and the treasure and Laddie; they even forgot where they were until they finished praying and got slowly to their feet.

"Where's Bob?" Mike asked quickly, looking about.

"I don't know," Danny said. "He was here a couple of minutes ago."

"I'll bet he's up to something."

At that instant they heard Laddie barking furiously from the direction of the creek. "Come on!" Danny cried. "Something's wrong!"

They went crashing through the woods to the water's edge just as Bob shoved out into the creek in the canoe. Laddie was running back and forth on shore and barking furiously.

"Now, let's see you sissies get home!" he cried.

The canoe was four or five feet from the bank when Laddie gave a mighty leap for it. He caught the side of the frail craft with his front feet. Bob screamed in terror as it flipped over, spilling him into the deep, churning water.

Chapter Eight

BOB CHANGES SOME IDEAS

"HELP!" Bob screamed as he went under. "Help!" He was thrashing the water wildly with his hands, and the current was taking him farther and farther from the bank. "Help! Help!"

"I'm coming!" Danny shouted, running down to the edge of the water.

Bob went under for the second time as Danny quickly kicked out of his shoes and dove into the deep, cold stream. Bob came up again, beating the water with his arms. The drowning lad clutched frantically for Dan, but the young woodsman eluded

"Is he dead?"

him, jackknifed in the water and came up behind Bob, grasping him by the hair before he realized what was happening. With his lungs gasping for air, Danny pulled Bob over to the bank where Mike was crouching.

"I got him!" Mike cried, reaching down and grabbing Bob beneath the arms. "I've got him!"

Danny scrambled up on the bank, and the two of them dragged Bob out of the water. He was unconscious now, and his pallid face was turning blue.

"Is he dead?" Mike gasped.

"Help me roll him over," Danny ordered. "We've got to get to work on him!"

"Bob!" Mike cried. "Open your eyes! Bob!"

Danny rolled Bob over on his stomach, laid the unconscious boy's head on one arm and began to work the water out.

"He took a lot of water," he explained as he worked over Bob. "We've got to get that out of him and get his lungs to working."

Mike watched in silence for a moment or two, then walked slowly over to where Laddie was lying, his head between his paws. The big dog seemed to sense the trouble he'd caused.

"That's all right, Laddie," Mike said softly. "That's all right, old fella."

He walked back, once more, to where Danny was working methodically over his brother. And without quite realizing what he was doing, he dropped to his knees and began to pray.

"O God," he prayed. "I—I don't know much about talking to You yet, but You know all about Bob. You know about this—this accident. You know about how he needs Your help. And the worst of it is, God, he isn't ready to die. He hasn't taken Jesus as his personal Saviour. O God, help Bob to be all right so he can become a Christian! And help him, Heavenly Father, to see that he needs Christ just as I did. In Jesus' name–" Mike wanted to pray more, but his voice choked until he couldn't go on. Instead he just knelt there in silence, his heart crying out to God. He didn't know how long he knelt there. Time seemed to stand still.

"Mike!" Danny said tensely. "Mike! He's moving!"

Sure enough! Bob's eyes opened, and he began to stir. The color had begun to come to his face. He was breathing in long gasps. While Mike watched, he struggled to roll over on his side. "O-o-o-h," he groaned.

"O God!" Mike cried. "I thank You! I do thank You."

Bob groaned again.

"Come on, Mike!" Danny ordered crisply. "We've got to get him in the house where it's warm."

Danny was shivering with the cold himself, but he was giving no thought to that. Together they carried Bob up to the house and laid him on the bed.

"You'd better trade clothes with him, Mike," Danny said as he saw that Bob was trembling with shock and cold. "Then we'll get this stove rigged up and get a fire going."

"Hadn't we better get him back to your place as quickly as we can?" Mike asked, peeling out of his shirt.

"We won't be able to do that tonight," Danny said. "Bob's in no shape to move, and besides, our canoe's floating downstream somewhere."

While Mike was getting Bob dressed in his own warm, dry clothes and crawling into the cold, wet shirt and trousers of his brother, Danny put the stovepipe back in the stove and chimney and got a fire going.

The wind came up again, moaning through the trees and whipping the usually quiet stream to a white-capped frenzy. Rain stung Danny's face as he carried in an armload of wood.

"We're really in for a storm," he said. "Let's move Bob in here in the kitchen and get these windows boarded up."

Bob got to his feet uncertainly and walked into the kitchen, holding on to the wall for support. Mike and Danny carried the slashed mattress in and laid it on the floor in front of the stove.

"I—I never did feel so weak," Bob said.

"You'd better lie down again," Danny told him, "while Mike and I get these windows covered up." Bob lay down, and Mike threw over him a piece of an old blanket he'd found in the corner of the closet.

It was beginning to get warm in the little kitchen, and by the time they had finished covering the windows it was very comfortable. Mike and Danny sat close to the fire so their clothes would dry.

"H-h-how're we going to get back to your place, Danny?" Mike asked softly when it seemed that Bob was asleep.

Danny shook his head. "I don't know," he said, "but God will take care of us. He'll help us get back, somehow. I'm not going to worry about it."

"I-I sure pulled a dumb one," Bob put in suddenly.

"I thought you were asleep," Mike explained.

"If it hadn't been for me, none of this would have

happened," he went on. "I had to go and get mad when you became a Christian a-a-and act like a fool."

"Everything worked out all right," Danny said. "That's the main thing."

"Well, thanks a lot for pulling me out, Danny," Bob said. "If you hadn't, I'd have been a goner. I—I can't swim at all."

"It was a good thing that we got you out when we did," Dan said. "You sure had swallowed a lot of water."

Bob had raised up on one elbow and was staring hard at his twin brother. There was a long silence.

"You—you were praying for me, weren't you?" he said at last, and so softly they could scarcely hear him.

Mike nodded without speaking.

"It seems sort of like a dream," he went on, "but I can kind of remember hearing you pray for me to be all right."

"God answered my prayer, Bob. At least He's answered half of it."

"Half of it. What do you mean?"

"I've been praying for you to take Jesus as your Saviour, just as hard as I prayed for Him to spare your life."

In the half-light Danny could see Bob biting his lower lip. "I—I know," he whispered. "I heard that too." He started to go on, but choked up and had to stop for a moment. "I've been fighting it ever since that first day on the boat when we were coming out to Angle Inlet. That was the reason I—I ran and tried to steal the canoe a-and leave you two stranded here. I knew that if I—I stayed around I—I'd be taking Christ as my Saviour, and I didn't want to. I didn't want to."

"I didn't want to either, Bob," Mike said quietly, "or at least I thought I didn't. It seemed to me like a Christian wouldn't ever have any fun." He stopped a moment, and a grin lighted his face. "I haven't been a Christian very long, but already I can see that I'm going to have more fun than I ever did."

"You know," Danny said, "if Satan can fool us that way and keep us from Christ, that's just what he wants to do."

"But I—I could never be good enough to be a Christian," Bob told him. "I say things I shouldn't, and swear and lie sometimes. There are so many things I do that a—a Christian shouldn't, that I just couldn't be good enough."

"Danny told me that being good in our own strength doesn't have anything to do with it," Mike put in. "If we confess our sins before Jesus, and put our trust in Him to save us and help us to keep from doing those things, it's all that's necessary. The Bible tells us that we can't be good enough on our own."

"But I like to go to shows and stuff like that," Bob countered.

"God can take care of that too," Danny said simply. "But you don't have to decide about everything like that now. Trying to do that is like trying to figure out exactly where you're going to place each foot every time you take a step on a ten-mile hike before you leave home. The main thing is to do like Mike said. Confess that you are a sinner who needs a Saviour, and put your trust in Him. After you've done that you can study your Bible and pray for guidance, and He will help you give up the things you shouldn't be doing."

There was another heavy silence. Finally Bob said,

"Would you pray with me, Mike?" His voice was thick with emotion.

The three of them knelt before the crackling fire while the rain beat against the roof, and the wind howled through the trees and rattled the door. Bob gave his heart to Christ. "O God," he prayed, "I'm — I'm a sinner, and—and please show me the way." When he finished and raised his head, there was a smile on his face that Mike had never seen before.

Soon after that it was dark, and Danny lit the stump of a candle he found in one of the cupboards. Then, taking out his water-soaked Testament, he read a couple of chapters, leaning close to the candle to catch its feeble light on the pages.

"It's funny," Bob said when they had finished reading, "but a fellow's ideas sure change fast. It used to make me mad when you'd read or even say anything about the Bible or Jesus. Now I like it."

They talked for a while and then went to sleep, curling up together on the old mattress.

The storm lasted all night long without a letup, and, toward morning Danny woke up, stiff and shivering. The fire had gone out, and the little kitchen was cold. He rolled over and propped himself up on one elbow.

"Is that you, Danny?" Bob asked, the moment he showed that he was awake.

"Yeah. I thought you were asleep."

"I'm so c-c-cold I can't sleep," Bob said. "For the last couple of hours I've about frozen to death."

"Me too," Danny said. "I'll see what I can do about that fire."

There was plenty of firewood in the house, but Danny had neglected to bring in any extra kindling.

71

"There are some old magazines in the other room," Bob said. "I saw them yesterday afternoon."

"I've got them," Danny said a moment later. "These'll make good kindling too." He threw a couple of dirty faded pictures with thin, veneer-like wood backing the frame on the floor before the stove.

He crumpled a double handful of magazine pages and put them in the stove, then knocked out the thin wood from the pictures and tossed the frames and the water-stained prints carelessly at Bob's feet. The fire flickered and leaped into flame.

A moment later Bob cried, "Danny! We've got it!" We've got it!"

"We've got what?" Danny demanded.

Mike sat up with a start, instantly awake.

"We've got it. We've got old Gibb's treasure map!"

Chapter Nine

THE STRANGERS' MAP

"WE'VE FOUND IT! We've found it!" Bob exclaimed over and over again, his voice trembling with excitement. "We've found the treasure map!"

"Are you sure?" Danny demanded.

"Of course, I'm sure. It couldn't be anything else!"

Danny and Mike crowded closer to him and peered over his shoulder in the flickering light. It was a map, glued to the back of the old-fashioned print of a basket of roses on a table. It was as faded and watersoaked as the picture it was glued to, but the lines were still sharp and clear. And down in the corner was the date and signature, *Renaud Du Bois, June 17, 1736.*

"It's the real thing all right," Danny said.

"Of course it's the real thing," Bob countered. "There's the signature of the guy who made it. It's even on some kind of skin instead of paper. Of course it's real."

Danny was studying the map and scarcely listening to the jabbering of his cousin. "There's the island Fort Charles used to be on," he said, pointing at a long, irregular shape on one side of the map. "This must be Massacre Island where that priest and the band of French soldiers were killed by the Indians."

"And here's where the treasure's buried," Mike cut

"It's the real thing all right!"

in, pointing to a small x along the western shore of Massacre Island.

"Oh, boy," Bob said, his whole body quivering with excitement. "Oh, boy, we can find the treasure now."

"First of all," Danny said soberly, "we've got to get out of here as quick as we can. Then we can think about looking for the treasure."

"But how're we going to get out of here?" Bob asked.

"We can't walk, that's a cinch," Mike put in. "There are at least three or four deep streams between here and Danny's place, to say nothing about having to make our way through eight or ten miles of forest and muskeg."

"We can't walk," Danny agreed, "but I've got my ax along, and I saw some heavy rope out in the woodshed. We can tie enough logs together with the rope to make a raft. It'll be slow going, but we can pole our way out of here. All we've got to do now is to wait until it gets light enough for us to work."

The boys sat there studying the map and talking, too excited to go back to sleep until daylight. With the coming of dawn the storm drifted southward, and the sun came up clear and warm.

Danny said as they stepped outside, the ax in his hands, "We haven't had anything to eat since yesterday noon. I'm getting powerful hungry."

"Eat?" Bob asked. "Who's got time enough to eat?"

"I have," Danny said. "There are some blueberries over there, Bob. Why don't you go over and pick some for us while Mike and I make the raft. We've got a lot of hard work ahead of us, and it might be another six or eight hours before we get a chance to eat again."

Danny and Mike cut down two or three straight, evenly shaped trees, trimmed off the branches, and cut the trunks into eight-foot lengths.

"Are you sure this'll hold the three of us and Laddie?" Mike asked as they lashed the last log into place and scooted the raft down into the water. "Sure it will," Danny said. "Our worry's going to be poling the thing, not drowning."

"The first mile and a half will be easy enough," Mike said, indicating the current they would be riding downstream.

"I know," Danny agreed, "but just wait until we have to buck the lake. There won't be any current there."

By the time they were ready to go, Bob was back with almost a gallon of big, juicy blueberries. "Say," he said, grinning, "these things are good. I didn't know how hungry I was until I got over in that patch."

"From the stains around your mouth and the looks of your face, you shouldn't be very hungry," Mike laughed good-naturedly.

They climbed aboard the raft, and Danny and Bob shoved it out into the current. The raft began to float slowly downstream.

"Now," Mike said, "Let me at some of those blueberries."

"I think we ought to have our morning devotions before we eat, don't you?" Danny asked.

"Sure thing," Bob said.

Danny opened his Testament to the Book of Psalms that was included in the back part of it and began to read from Psalm 98. "O sing unto the LORD a new song; for he hath done marvellous things:...The LORD hath made known his salvation."

"God has sure done that on this trip," Mike broke in. "He's made known His salvation so plain and clear to Bob and me that we couldn't run away from it. We had to accept Him as our Saviour."

"I was just thinking the same thing," Bob said.

When Danny finished reading, all three of them prayed in turn, thanking God that Mike and Bob had found Christ as their Saviour, thanking Him for caring for Bob in time of danger and for watching over them through the stormy night.

"And, O Lord," Danny concluded, "bless this food as we eat it and help us to use the strength we receive to Thine honor and glory. In Jesus' name. Amen."

They were still eating blueberries and talking excitedly about the map when Mike spied the canoe floating upside down along shore.

"Look!" he cried. "There's our canoe!"

Quickly they poled the clumsy raft over alongside the canoe.

"Boy, this is swell!" Danny said as he grabbed hold of the canoe. "I've been wondering how we were ever going to pole this raft all the way to our place, and what I was going to tell Dad about losing the canoe. It's the best one we've got."

"God does watch over a fellow, doesn't He?" Bob said as they bailed the water out of the canoe and got into it.

"Yes," Danny said. "The important thing is to just keep our trust in Him and to remember that all things work together for good to them who love Him."

One paddle had been washed away when Bob and Laddie upset the canoe, but Danny had two others lashed securely in the canoe. They unfastened them quickly and began to paddle.

They had not been paddling more than fifteen or twenty minutes when they heard the high-pitched whine of an outboard motor.

"Somebody's coming," Bob said excitedly. "Ditch that map!"

"I've got it," Mike said, "and no one'll ever find it."

"That sounds like your dad's motor, Danny," Bob went on. "Do you suppose it's Cliff and Jack coming after us?"

"It's more likely Dad," Danny said. "He and Mother have probably been worried silly with that bad storm and us not showing up all night."

It was Danny's dad in the boat alone, his gray hat pulled low over his eyes.

"Now, where have you fellows been?" he asked as he cut the motor and pulled alongside of them. "Your mother's been about crazy with worry, Danny. She didn't sleep at all last night. And neither did I."

"I know," Danny said when they had paddled to shore and transferred into the aluminum boat. "But there just wasn't anything we could do about it." Hurriedly he told what had happened.

"Well," Mr. Orlis said, "we can thank God that you're all safe."

"We have something else to thank God for, Uncle Carl," Bob said. "Both Mike and I took Christ as our Saviour last night."

"Well, now that's something." The big man smiled broadly. "That's wonderful."

Back home Danny's mother cried a little, kissed all

three of them and fixed them the biggest breakfast they'd ever seen in all their lives. While they were eating, Cliff and Jack came sauntering in.

"There are the fellows that stayed out all night," Jack said, trying to laugh and sound friendly. "What happened to you, anyway?"

"We got caught out in the storm," Danny said.

"We were out scouting around a little yesterday too," he went on, "but we didn't see you."

"Well," Danny replied, "the Lake of the Woods is pretty big."

"That storm was a long time coming up," Jack went on, eying the boys carefully. "It must've been something pretty important to keep you out when clouds like those were threatening."

"It was something mighty important," Bob said without thinking. "And what's more we got what we went after too." The instant he spoke the color began to rise in his cheeks. Danny and Mike both looked up at him quickly.

"Oh," Jack said, getting to his feet, "I see." He started for the door. "Come on, Cliff. We'd better get to circulating."

There was no chance for the boys to get away from the place to look for the treasure that day, not after having stayed out the night before. Danny helped his mother clean the cabins, and Mike and Bob got ice out of the ice house and cut a pile of firewood and carried water for the chickens and rabbits. It was after supper, and they were back in their cabin alone before they had a chance to talk to one another.

"Boy," Bob said, "I sure spilled things this noon. I could've cut my tongue out when I realized what I'd said."

"It probably set them to wondering, all right." Danny said, "but I don't think you gave them enough information to really give them a line on anything."

"We'll have to be extra careful now, though," Mike said. "If they get wind of the map, we'll be in the soup."

Bob sighed. "I sure hope they didn't find out enough to do them any good."

"Right now we've got something else to worry about," Danny said as he dumped a handful of paper scraps on the table.

"What's this?" Mike asked.

"That's what we've got to find out. I found them out in back of Jack and Cliff's cabin this afternoon."

Bob went over and pulled the blinds while Mike and Danny began to fit the pieces together.

"Why, it's a map," Danny said in a moment or two. "A map of Angle Inlet."

"It sure is. And it's got a treasure marked on it!" Mike exclaimed. "Right over there on the mainland."

They stared at the torn pieces, wondering. "I can see why someone would come up here to hunt for a treasure with a map," Danny said. "But I can't see why they would tear the map up after they got here."

"This map doesn't look very old to me," Bob said, "not like ours does anyway. I'll bet it isn't real."

"We know it can't be the real map," Danny told him, "because we've got it."

They sat there looking at one another. "It just doesn't make sense," Mike said.

That night when they went to bed, Bob just could not sleep. He kept thinking of how he almost drowned, and would have, if Danny hadn't pulled him out; how he had become a Christian there in Gibb McCloud's old house; how they had found the map they had gone after; and how Danny had found the mysterious map which had been torn to shreds.

He was lying there quite still, but very wide awake when he heard a muffled footstep on the porch. Instantly his eyes were open, striving to pierce the darkness. There was a long, breathless silence, and the doorknob began to turn. He could not see it, but he could hear the thin sound of metal against metal as the catch was drawn. Somebody was on the porch. Somebody was breaking into their cabin!

Chapter Ten

A NIGHT PROWLER

THERE WAS A LONG, deathly silence in the little cabin while Bob lay there, wide-eyed, and not daring to move. Somebody was going to break into the cabin, and he lay there helpless. There wasn't a thing he could do. He heard the door catch click. In the hush of the night it sounded like a rifle bullet, and the guarded noises on the other side of the door froze instantly.

They should have locked that door, especially after they had found the map and he'd made such a break in front of Cliff and Jack. They should have hidden the map someplace besides under Danny's mattress. Bob could hear Mike and Danny breathing regularly, but they were across the cabin. There was no way of waking them without warning the intruder.

The door began to move slowly, and he heard a muffled footstep on the threshold, the faint creak of shoe leather against the wood floor.

"O God," Bob prayed fervently, "help me to know what to do." He reached out for the table that stood beside his bed, his groping fingers at last encircling something solid.

The door opened a little wider, and he could faintly make out the heavy bulk of someone against the moonlight as the intruder moved silently inside. Bob

*"He could faintly make out the heavy bulk of some-
one against the moonlight.*

straightened suddenly and threw a perfect strike toward the big shape in the doorway. There was a thud, a loud, terrifying yell, and the strong odor of kerosene.

"Mike! Danny!" Bob cried, "Wake up!"

They were both awake instantly.

"What happened, Bob?" Mike asked. "What's the matter? What's wrong?"

"W-w-w-what's the matter?" Danny asked tensely.

"The map?" Bob asked. "Is it there?"

Danny felt under the mattress.

"Sure it is, why?"

"Somebody's after it, guys," Bob said hoarsely. "I heard him come in a couple of minutes ago. He was right inside this cabin!"

"Nobody'd break into the cabin while we were here," Danny said. "They'd know that they would never be able to get away with it."

"I don't know about that," Bob went on, "but I do know he was in here, and I let him have it with the first thing I could get my hands on."

"I think you were just having a nightmare, Bob," Danny laughed.

"But I saw him, I tell you. I threw the lamp at him."

"That was the man in the moon," Mike said.

"Just the same," Bob countered, "I'll bet he's got a black eye."

Even though they laughed at Bob, both Mike and Danny lay in bed for a long while without sleep. Finally all three of them drifted off to sleep, waking with a start at the slightest sound. When the first faint rays of dawn began to lighten the horizon, Bob got up and swung his feet over the side of the bed.

Danny's Testament was there. He picked it up and looked at it. It was the first time in his life that he'd actually held a Testament because he wanted to, because he was looking for something to read. It was still wet from the dunking Danny had given it the day before when he had pulled Bob out of the river. He turned the well-worn pages slowly. Danny had underlined much of it.

"Whosoever therefore shall confess me before men, him will I confess also before my Father which is in heaven." That verse was clear enough. He was glad he'd confessed Christ before men. Over in Mark there was part of a verse that Danny had underlined, "For with God all things are possible." For a moment or two Bob closed the Testament and looked across the room. To think, he had a God like that, a God who could do anything. Bob fingered the Testament lovingly. And that wonderful God had provided salvation free to any who would receive it. All he had to do was to confess his sins and put his trust in Christ. While he was sitting there, he heard the door to the next cabin close, and a moment later Cliff and Jack came walking past.

"I never will get the smell of kerosene out of my clothes," Cliff was saying. "You told me those kids would be sleeping in the house last night."

"I thought they would be."

"Well, the next time you can do your own prowling."

When Bob told Danny and Mike about it, Danny said, "Now don't go to giving us any more of that stuff."

"You guys wouldn't believe anything."

When they went into the house for breakfast that morning, Bob took one look at Cliff and punched Danny in the ribs, hard. The short one's left eye was swelled shut and was as black as Danny's pet crow.

"I—I ran into something in the dark last night," Cliff explained lamely, when he saw that the three boys were staring at him.

"Yes," Jack said, laughing, "that door'll never be the same again."

The two men ate hurriedly and, without excusing themselves, got up and left the house before Danny's father began the morning's devotions.

"Well, now," Mr. Orlis said when they were gone. "I wonder what got into them."

In a moment or two the outboard started with a roar and went speeding downstream.

"I'm going to talk to them about that," Danny's dad said, his eyes narrowing. "I don't like the idea of having my boats taken without permission."

As soon as the Bible reading and prayer were over, Danny and the twins excused themselves and went out to the canoe.

"Have you got the map?" Mike asked as they stood on the dock.

Danny nodded. "I brought Dad's binoculars too. They might come in handy if Cliff and Jack are really after us."

"What do you mean, really after us?" Bob countered. "You saw Cliff's eye, didn't you?"

"I guess I've got to admit it wasn't a pipe dream this time," Danny said. "But I still can't figure out what they're up to."

"Neither can I," Mike said, "but whatever it is, we know that for us at least it isn't good."

"Let's forget those fellows for a while," Bob said, "and take a good look at that map. Just where is it that we go, Danny?"

"Down toward Penasse on American Point," Danny said, "to Massacre Island. We came right past it as we came in on the boat from Warroad."

"Sure," Mike put in. "I remember it. You pointed it out to us."

"If this direction is north," Danny said pointing, "then we'll have to go over to the southwest corner of the island and leave our canoe. According to the map, the treasure is buried quite a way back on the island, back on that little ridge that runs along it."

They paddled on for half an hour or more, not rapidly, but with long, firm strokes that sent the little canoe rippling through the water.

"Say, Danny," Bob said at last, "you had a verse in your Testament marked that said something about your body being a living sacrifice. What'd that mean?"

"What book was it in?" Danny asked.

"I don't know for sure. It was somewhere in the middle."

Danny thought for a moment. "That must have been Romans." He stopped paddling a moment, got out his Testament, and turned to the twelfth chapter of Romans. "Does this sound like it? 'I beseech you therefore, brethren, by the mercies of God, that ye present your bodies a living sacrifice, holy, acceptable unto God, which is your reasonable service?' "

"Yeah, that's the one. What does it mean?"

"Well," Danny began, "it means that when Jesus

comes into our hearts, He wants to take possession of our bodies too. Our bodies become Christ's home here on earth."

Bob was silent a moment or two. "That's how you get that a Christian shouldn't smoke or drink or do anything that would harm his body, isn't it?" he asked.

"That's one of the verses," Danny said.

Mike, who had been watching the horizon as he listened, reached over and picked up the field glasses and trained them on a dark spot along the shore of one of the islands.

"Take a look over there, Danny," he said at last. "Doesn't that look like your boat?"

Danny looked through the glasses. "It is," he said. "I wonder what they're doing over there."

"I'll bet they're watching us," Bob put in.

Danny swung the canoe about abruptly and headed north along the shore of Massacre Island. "We'll soon see," he said. While he and Bob paddled furiously, Mike kept the glasses trained on them.

"They're following us, all right," he said. "And one of them looks like he's got a pair of field glasses on us."

"What're we going to do?" Bob asked. "They've really got it over us with that motor boat. They can catch us any time they want."

For answer Danny thrust his paddle deep in the water and turned the canoe toward shore.

"They can't catch us if they can't see us," he said, laughing. "The island's narrow here. We'll portage the canoe to the other side, put it in the water and paddle to where we want to go. They'll never know what happened to us."

The boys paddled into a little cove that gave them momentary protection from the prying eyes of the field glasses, hauled the feather-light canoe up onto the shore and began to carry it through the trees. The forest was dense, but it took only a few minutes to carry the canoe across the narrow length of the island and launch it in the lake once more.

"I'd give a lot to see the look on Cliff's face when they come buzzing up to the other side and start to look for us," Bob laughed.

"Let's get going," Mike said nervously. "They might come around on this side and catch us."

The boys kept looking around, half fearfully, as they paddled furiously toward the south end of the island. They could hear the outboard motor making its way up and down the other side of Massacre Island, and once or twice, the boys held their breath, expecting the boat to come around on the east side. But finally the high-pitched whine began to fade away.

"They're heading for home," Danny said happily. "Now let's get to that treasure!"

They studied the map and left the canoe at the point nearest to the spot where the treasure was supposed to be buried and began to make their way through the trees to the top of the ridge.

"I think we're a little too far to the right," Danny said when they stopped for breath. "I don't see anything up here that looks like a granite boulder with a jagged point on top."

"We should have brought a compass along," Mike said.

"A spade!" Bob broke in suddenly. "We came clear over here to dig for a treasure and didn't bring a spade!"

"Oh, well," Bob said good-naturedly, "we can look for the granite boulder today and come back tomorrow and dig."

Danny could not help thinking, as they began to walk along the ridge, about how different Bob had become since he'd accepted Christ as his Saviour. Before, he'd have jumped down Danny's throat about that spade. He'd have blamed him for it and blamed Mike for it and would have raved until both of them would have felt like throwing him in the lake. Now he just said that they could come back tomorrow. Yes, sir, becoming a Christian sure did things to a person.

As things turned out they couldn't have used the spade anyway, for though they hunted until it hurried them to get home in time for supper, they didn't find a sign of the boulder.

"You don't suppose somebody moved it, do you?" Bob asked as they nosed the canoe into the shore in front of their cabin.

"Sure," Danny laughed. "They carried it out piggy-back."

Mike was the first one to go into their cabin. He stopped in the doorway and whistled in amazement.

"Danny! Bob!" he cried. "Come here, quick! Somebody's upset our beds, and dresser drawers and everything. They've turned our cabin inside out!"

Chapter Eleven

DANNY TO THE RESCUE

"WOULD YOU LOOK at this mess!" Danny exclaimed as he stood in the middle of the little cabin floor and looked about.

"I knew they'd be back!" Bob said excitedly. "I knew when they tried to break in last night that they'd be back!"

"It's the map they're after," Danny said as though the possibility had just occurred to him.

"Sure, it's the map," Mike said. "They've found out that we've got it, and they're out to get it away from us if they can."

"And," Danny added darkly, "I don't think they care how they do it, either."

"They'll likely be back again tonight, guys," he said, "if we don't do something."

Danny crossed over and closed the door. "There's not much we can do about their coming back if they decide to," he said. "What we've got to do is get the map put away where they can't get at it, even if they do come back for it."

"What if they force their way in and make us tell where it is?" Bob asked.

"That's a chance we'll have to take," Danny replied.

They slipped out into the woods, one after the

other, and met just beyond the old sawmill on the edge of the path to the schoolhouse.

"Are you sure neither of you were followed?" Danny asked Mike and Bob when all three of them were together once more.

"Nope," Bob said. "Nobody followed me."

"Nobody followed me, either," Mike said. "I slipped out through the back window in the cow barn."

"Well," Danny said. "I don't think Cliff and Jack are around, but we can't take any chances."

"That's right," Bob put in, "but now that we're out here like you said, what're we going to do?"

"First of all we're going to hide this map so they can never find it," Danny said. "Then we're going to get our things together so we can get out early in the morning, before Cliff and Jack are even up."

Mike looked about quickly. "This doesn't look like much of a place to hide a map."

"It's a lot better than around the house or one of the buildings," Bob said.

"That's the way I figured," Danny went on. "There's a hollow log up here a little ways. It isn't so far out of the way for us to come to pick up the map in the morning, and if they didn't follow us out here, they'd never be able to find it."

Once the precious map was safely hidden in the hollow tree, the boys went back to the cabin and got the equipment together that they figured they would need. Bob dug a compass out of his suitcase. Danny brought a spade and a length of good, strong rope from the woodshed.

"Now," he said, "we'll have Mom fix lunch for us, and we'll be all set to leave tomorrow."

The dinner bell just outside the kitchen door clanged loudly, and Mike got to his feet. "Come on," he said. "I'm about starved."

"Remember," Danny warned, "let's not say anything at all about our cabin being ransacked. Let's just go in and act as though nothing happened."

At the doorway to the main house Danny paused.

"Say, Carl," said the skipper of the boat that was tied at Angle Inlet for the night. "Whatever's come over that loud-mouthed, ornery kid I hauled up here awhile back. I've noticed on my last trip or so that he doesn't act like the same boy any more."

"How do you mean?" Danny's dad asked, smiling.

"Well," the boat captain went on, "he isn't shooting off at the mouth all the time. He's got a smile and a kind word for everyone now and—I don't know how to explain it. He just acts like a different guy."

"Why don't you ask him what came over him?" Mr. Orlis suggested. "He's on the porch right now."

When Bob stepped inside, Mr. Orlis turned to him. "Bob," he said, "the skipper here has been wondering what's come over you. He says you don't act like the same boy that came up here."

"I guess I'm not," Bob said evenly, and without conceit. "You see I've taken Christ as my Saviour since I came up here. Any difference that you see in me is because of Him. I—I'm not perfect by a long way, and I prob'ly never will be, but I'm just putting my trust in Christ to help me live the kind of life He wants me to."

The skipper picked up his glass and took a long drink of water.

"I've knowed you to talk about the change that becoming a Christian can make, Carl," he said slowly,

95

"but this is the first time I've ever seen it happen right before my eyes."

The boys were sitting at the table before they noticed that there were two empty chairs.

"Where're Cliff and Jack?" Danny asked, striving to be casual.

"If they can't get here for mealtime," Mr. Orlis said shortly, "they can just go hungry. I'm getting mighty tired of those two fellows coming in here and trying to take over."

They had finished eating and were sitting in the living room talking when they heard the outboard motorboat come in and stop at the dock.

Mr. Orlis looked at his watch fifteen or twenty minutes later. "That's funny," he said. "I thought sure those two would be in here crying for something to eat long before this." He reached over and got the checkerboard and set it on the table between himself and the boat captain. "There's something mysterious about Cliff and Jack, and I don't like it. I've a good notion to send them on their way in a day or two."

Bob started to say something, but Danny kicked him on the shins.

The next morning the boys were up even earlier than they had been the day before. They dressed in the semidarkness of early morning, and Bob and Mike quietly loaded the canoe while Danny slipped out into the woods to get the map.

"Did you get it?" Bob whispered guardedly as he approached a few minutes later.

"Yep," he said, smiling. "It was just as safe as could be. Have you got everything?"

Mike checked carefully and said, "It looks like it's all here this time."

"Fine."

"Now," Bob said softly, "if we can just get out of here and over to the island without having anyone see us."

While the other two boys and Danny's dog, Laddie, were getting into the canoe, Danny looked about carefully, his dark eyes piercing the semidarkness. There was an eerie fog that hung like a shroud over the lake.

"The boat Cliff and Jack have been using is here, all right," Danny said, his voice growing suddenly tense. "But one of the canoes is gone."

Bob and Mike straightened quickly.

"W-w-what do you suppose happened to it?" Mike asked as though he didn't know the answer.

"Cliff and Jack have got it," Bob put in quickly.

"They just couldn't have gotten out earlier than we did this morning," Danny went on. "They must have left last night."

"Then they're out there," Bob said excitedly. "They're out on the lake somewhere just waiting for us!"

"What're we going to do?" Mike asked.

Danny stepped lightly into the canoe and shoved it away from the dock. "We'd better get going just as fast as we can," he said, "to take advantage of this fog. As long as it holds out, they can't see us."

"But we can't see them, either," Bob exclaimed.

They wielded their lithe Indian paddles expertly, and the light canoe knifed silently through the water, sending a widening V of ripples across the smooth surface. It was cold out on the big northern Minnesota lake, but the paddling soon warmed them. For three or four miles they paddled over water as smooth and motionless as a marble floor under fog so thick they couldn't make out either shore.

"We ought to be getting pretty close to Massacre Island, hadn't we?" Mike said softly as they paused to rest.

"It isn't too far," Danny told him.

"We've been lucky so far," Bob put in. "Now if we can just make it the rest of the way safely we'll be O.K."

Laddie moved a little, and Danny reached out and patted the big dog lovingly on the head. "We'll be there in a little while, old man," he said.

"You know," Bob said, "if we find the treasure, I've just thought of something that I'd like to see us do."

"What's that?" Mike asked, "go to Florida?"

"Nope," he went on. "I've been thinking about that schoolhouse we have to use for a church. I—I know it doesn't matter what kind of a building we worship in, but I kind of figure that if we had us a nice little church that really looked like a church on the inside, it might help us to worship God better. It might even make us so proud of it that we'd try to get a minister to come up and serve us. Then something could be done about people like Rick Thunderbird and the other Indians and white people who live up here and who have never heard about Jesus."

Mike and Danny just sat there for a moment or two looking at one another.

"You know," Danny said at last, "you make me ashamed of myself, Bob. Here I've been thinking about what I could do for myself, and you, who haven't even been a Christian very long, had to show me what I'd ought to be thinking about. You've got a swell idea there."

"I think so too," Mike added.

The boys pulled their canoe up on shore and hid it in the brush that grew along the lake.

"You fellows go ahead with the map and compass and go right toward the place where the treasure's supposed to be buried," Danny said. "I'll take this load of stuff up to that pine tree where we were yesterday and make camp. Then I'll join you, and we'll really get to work."

"That sounds good," Bob exclaimed taking the wrinkled, faded map out of the canoe.

The twins went ahead, half running through the trees, while Danny gathered up the equipment and lunch and began to trudge, with Laddie at his side, up the steep ridge.

The load was heavy and awkward, and he stopped several times to rest. It took him almost half an hour to get up to the big pine tree. He was just setting down the spade and rope when he heard a loud, blood-chilling scream.

He froze instantly! The hair on the back of Laddie's neck raised, and the big dog growled and took a step or two toward the sound.

There it was again! "Help! Danny! Help! Help!" Danny's heart throbbed in his throat. Bob and Mike were in trouble!

Chapter Twelve

THE REAL TREASURE

DANNY ORLIS stood there a moment, icicles playing up and down his spine. The scream had come from the direction Bob and Mike had gone a few minutes before. Somebody must have grabbed them! While he stood there, too frightened to move, the scream came again, a terrifying scream. "Help! Danny! Help!"

The hair raised ominously on the back of Laddie's neck. The muscles in his shoulders tightened as though he were ready to spring upon someone.

"Easy, boy," Danny whispered hoarsely, laying his hand on the big dog's back. "Easy now, fellow."

Even before the scream died away, Danny knew what had happened. Jack and Cliff had figured that the boys would be coming back to Massacre Island, so the two hoodlums had sneaked away from Angle Inlet by canoe and had hidden themselves on the island to wait for them. Now they had the map and Mike and Bob and everything!

Laddie inched forward, his ears laid back against his head, and a low, deep-throated growl escaped his razor-sharp teeth. Danny took hold of one ear gently. "Easy, fellow. Easy now." The dog relaxed a little, but kept peering sharply into the woods in the direction from which the screams had come.

A breathless hush seemed to settle over the island, enveloping Danny like a cloud. His own deep breathing was the only sound he could hear. He took a step forward, and a twig crackled. He jumped back, startled. His heart was beating faster now, and his breath was coming in short gasps. If only he could turn and run! If only he could flee the island before Jack and Cliff got him too!

Suddenly he was ashamed of himself, ashamed of even thinking that he could go away and leave Mike and Bob in the hands of those two men.

He dropped slowly to his knees and buried his hands and face in Laddie's broad back.

"O Heavenly Father," he prayed, "just be with Mike and Bob and keep them from any harm. And, O God, help me to figure out something to do—quickly."

He didn't know how long he knelt there. It might have been two minutes. It might have been ten or fifteen minutes. But before he got to his feet, a quiet assurance came over him. He was still scared, so scared that the palms of his hands were wet with sweat, so scared his heart was thumping like a trip hammer, but now he had control of himself. He knew that God was there to help him. "And, O Heavenly Father," he prayed in conclusion, "I do thank Thee that both Mike and Bob have found Thee as their personal Saviour. In Jesus' name, I pray. Amen."

He got to his feet slowly. The first thing to do would be to get over there where Jack and Cliff held the twins captive. If he could make that without being seen, he could figure out something from there. He went through the stuff he had carried from the canoe. His hunting knife was strapped to his belt, and he found a long length of rope and a sharp ax, but that was all. Quickly he picked them up and began to walk toward the screams.

His experience in the woods served him well as he made his way across the ridge searching for Mike and Bob. He stepped quickly, but silently, his gaze darting about the forest ahead, picking up every shadow, every flickering movement. He stopped frequently, his keen ears alert for any sound of voices or feet, or the chattering of birds or squirrels that would reveal the presence of men. He stalked through the forest like an Indian, sharp-eyed and cautious, every step of the way. Laddie seemed to sense what he was doing and pressed close beside him, his feet padding silently over the moss.

He had walked half a mile or so, when he heard a sound in the trees just ahead. Laddie heard it first. The dog's ears went up instantly, and he stopped, his nose thrust forward to catch the scent. Danny froze where he was as the hair on the dog's neck began to bristle. The sound was faint and indistinct, but it was there. They were somewhere just ahead. His heart started racing again as he began to steal forward, a step at a time, an unspoken prayer on his lips.

With every step the sounds seemed louder. In a moment or two he could make out Cliff and Jack's voices. They were talking fast and loud.

Danny stood for a moment. There was no telling what he would find as he stepped closer. He might step out into a clearing and meet them face to face. He might stumble over a dead branch or fall over a rock and get caught before he ever saw Mike and Bob, let alone rescue them. He might—but there was no time to think of things like that. He dropped to his stomach and began to wriggle forward. Laddie did likewise, crawling close to the ground.

"I'll tell you, Jack, we'd ought to go out and look for

that other kid first," Cliff was saying angrily, "and look for the treasure afterwards. He's loose on this island, and there's no telling what he'll do."

"Don't tell me you're getting scared of a kid," Jack snorted. "Come on over here with that mine detector and let's get to work."

"O.K., O.K." said Cliff.

Danny pressed even closer to the ground and began to inch forward. He could see them now, going over the ground with that queer-looking contraption he'd seen in their cabin. And, beyond them some twenty or thirty feet, he could see Mike and Bob, tied securely and gagged.

"Take another look at that map, will you?" Cliff complained. "It doesn't seem to me that we're in the right place."

Jack studied the map they had stolen from the twins. "You'd better go five or six paces to—" Before he could finish what he was saying, the mine detector began to click wildly.

"We've found it! We've found it!" Cliff cried loudly throwing aside the mine detector and dropping to his knees over the spot where the machine had indicated metal.

"Get out of the way and let me in there with that spade!" Jack exclaimed, pushing his partner aside. "Get that other spade, and let's get to digging!"

They began to dig madly in the hard, rocky soil, hacking at the ground with the spade and clawing at the tree roots with the dull hatchet they had brought along.

For two or three minutes Danny watched them in their frenzied efforts to get down to the treasure. Then he turned and began to crawl around the narrow clearing to where Bob and Mike were tied. He moved quietly, always keeping a screen of trees between himself and the men, but they were too excited, too wild for gold, to hear anything. They were both trying to dig at once, and every now and then their spades would ring as they clanged together.

Danny slipped up behind the twins, slit the ropes that bound their hands and feet.

"S-s-sh," he whispered from behind the tree. "Are you ready?"

They both nodded grimly.

Cliff and Jack had dug a hole about knee deep and two or three feet across. One of them was standing in the hole, and the other was bending over it, working so hard the sweat ran down his face and soaked through his shirt.

The dog sprang across the little clearing.

"Laddie," Danny whispered to the dog crouched beside him, "Sic 'em! Sic 'em!"

The big dog let out a growl and sprang across the little clearing, hitting Jack squarely in the middle of the back with his front feet. The startled man went sprawling into the hole on top of his companion, and they both went down in a heap with the snarling, biting dog on top of them. An instant later the three boys jumped into the fray, and before Cliff and Jack realized what had happened, Danny, Mike and Bob had them securely tied. Both of the men were screaming loudly. "Call off the dog!" they cried. "Call him off! Call him off!"

"Down, Laddie!" Danny ordered, and the dog dropped back instantly, and without growling; but his shoulders were tense, and his eyes never left the two men.

"Boy, you came just in time," Bob gasped when the excitement was over and they had the two men tied to a tree.

"Yes, the Lord certainly guided me this morning," Danny said.

"You know," Bob went on, "we weren't too worried and scared. We both kept praying all the time."

"We were praying that you'd be able to set us free, only we didn't expect you quite so quick."

"Well," Danny asked, smiling as he saw that Cliff and Jack were staring angrily at him, "do you suppose that mine detector really found the treasure?"

"There's no time like now to find out," Bob said, picking up a spade.

"Here, I'll help you," Danny said. "Watch 'em, Laddie."

The big dog planted himself squarely before the two men and growled every time one of them moved.

"Don't sic him on us again," Cliff pleaded. "We won't try to get away. Honest we won't. Only don't sic him on us again."

"You just behave yourself, and you and Laddie'll get along fine," Danny said. "But don't try any funny stuff, or he'll jump right in the middle of you."

The first time Bob thrust the spade in the ground it hit something solid.

"I—I hit something!" he said excitedly.

Mike grabbed up the other spade and began to dig too, and in a twinkling, they had uncovered a small rusty box.

"That's it!" Danny cried.

"We've found it! We've found it!" Mike and Bob both echoed together.

"Here," Danny said. "I'll give you a hand!" It was all the three of them could do to lift it out of the hole.

"Hurry up!" Bob exclaimed. "Let's get it opened up and see what it is!"

"I'm afraid we're going to have to wait until we get it back to Angle Inlet to do that," Danny replied. "Look at that padlock. We haven't got anything along that can break that."

"Here," Bob said. "Let me see it." He whacked it a dozen times with the hatchet but couldn't dent the tough metal. "I guess you're right."

Laddie guarded the prisoners while the boys carried the treasure down and loaded it into the big canoe which Jack and Cliff had stolen. Then they got the men and the dog and towed all three in the second canoe back to Angle Inlet.

"Aren't you afraid they'll get away?" Mike asked when Danny ordered them into the canoe.

"Not with Laddie along," Danny said.

"Nor with their hands tied, either," Bob added. "They aren't going to want to get out of that canoe when their hands are tied so they can't swim."

Back at Angle Inlet the boys found Danny's mother and father, and a Royal Canadian Mountie, and the crew of the boat standing on the dock waiting for them. The mountie's fast speedboat was idling at the end of the dock.

"Another five minutes and we'd have been out there after you boys," Mr. Orlis said as they docked. "We were just going to gas up the speedboat and go."

"They're the troublemakers," the Mountie exclaimed. "That's them, all right. They've made a racket of going into a territory and making fake treasure maps to sell to unsuspecting people, maps like those we found in their cabin."

"We found a real treasure map," Bob said. "We've got the treasure to prove it!"

They all gathered about while Mr. Orlis broke the lock with a crow bar.

"Gold!" Mike and Bob exclaimed. "Gold!"

"I—I guess we've got enough to build our church now," Danny stammered excitedly.

"I guess so," Bob said. "And some to spend for missions and still have enough left for ourselves."

Later, after the Mountie had loaded Jack and Cliff into his boat and roared off across the lake, Bob said to Mike and Danny, "You know, it was something to find that treasure. But the treasure isn't the most important thing I found up here at Angle Inlet. The important Person I found up here is the Lord Jesus Christ, my personal Saviour."

Mike was silent for a long while. "I guess you're right about that," he said at last.

Danny looked up at them and grinned. "I've been praying for you two guys ever since I heard you were coming up here to spend the summer," he said. "And if I'd had to take my choice, I'd have taken you two as Christians any day before I'd have taken my share of the treasure."

"But God gave us both salvation and the treasure," Bob said. "I guess that just goes to show how He does bless if we try to be faithful." And, there on the floor of the little cabin, the three of them knelt in prayer, thanking God for His goodness to them.

For a complete list of available books, write to:
Sword of the Lord Publishers
P. O. Box 1099
Murfreesboro, Tennessee 37133.

(800) 251-4100
(615) 893-6700
FAX (615) 848-6943
www.swordofthelord.com